ISBN 978-1-7320512-6-3

Published in large print in 2024 by Delphi Books

The text of this Large Print edition is unabridged. Other aspects of the book may vary from the original edition.

Set in 16 pt. Plantin

Printed in the United States on permanent paper.

# Miss Priss
## AND THE
# Pirate

# FRAN BAKER

**DELPHI BOOKS**

*For Louie*

*Until we meet again, Édesem*

## Chapter 1

Cornwall
1817

*P*riscilla "Priss" Fitch pulled out a piece of paper from her desk drawer, dipped her pretty ostrich plume pen in the ink pot, and began to write:

*The Caribbean*
*1702*

"Ship ahoy!" Sunlight sparked off the sailor's spyglass as he scanned the horizon from the crow's nest. "Broad on the port bow!"

While none of his mates actually stopped working to look, there was an unspoken ripple of alertness among both the crew and the isolated groups of passengers on the deck of the merchantman *James Bond.*

Victoria Gordon joined the other

passengers gathering at the rail. At eighteen years of age, she was a small, neat young woman clad in light brown linen, unadorned with either lace or jewels. Instead of the tortured curls that were considered fashionable, her thick brown hair had been pulled back from her face and confined in a plump coil at the nape of her neck. Her appearance suggested exactly what she was—a French convent-schooled graduate who was returning from Martinique to her widowed father's London home, where it was expected that she would meet and marry some eligible gentleman.

Now, she shaded her eyes against the prickly glare of sun on sea with a properly gloved hand and focused on the jagged line of the horizon. It didn't help as much as she had hoped. She could see nothing but flat blue miles of water.

"She still approaching?" The captain, standing a few feet behind Victoria, startled her as he bellowed up at the sailor in the crow's nest.

"Yessir," the sailor yelled down.

"What flag does she fly?" the captain demanded.

"English, sir."

A relieved murmur spread like a gentle wave among the passengers at the news. The crew got on with their duties but remained on the alert for further developments.

Nearly sun-blinded by now Victoria blinked several times to clear her vision before she resumed peering into the distance. Finally, she saw a smudge on the horizon. A smudge that eventually took the shape of a ship that was slowly traveling toward the *James Bond.*

"She's taking in the situation," a male passenger to her left pointed out.

"Her sails are furled," another man said, a little too sharply.

"What does that mean?" Victoria asked them.

Neither they nor any of the other passengers answered her. They were all staring in blank bewilderment at the oncoming vessel, not yet understanding what was taking place.

Sea spray stung Victoria's face when she dropped her hand and watched the sleek, unidentified ship move steadily toward the *James Bond.* It took its time, breasting the foamy waves and nudging the wind as it neared. Still too far away to show more than its flag and iron-sheathed bow, the approaching ship began lining up at a point directly in front of the *James Bond* and its gaping passengers.

"Notice how they're angling in toward our bow so we can't fire on them?" the portly man to Victoria's right observed.

"Why would they do that?" she asked him.

He was rescued from response by his frothy wife, who stood on his other side fluttering her fan. "Oh, me, oh, my," she stewed. "You don't suppose they're—"

The other ship's sails burst open then, rendering her into shocked silence as they unfurled with a *whoosh* of wind-billowed black canvas.

"They're lowering the British Jack!" cried the sailor in the crow's nest. "They're raising—they're raising the—"

Victoria clutched the rail with frozen fingers as she watched the black-and-white Jolly Roger fly up the ship's flag line.

And then everyone understood.

"Pirates!" shrieked a sailor.

*Chapter 2*

―∽∽―

"*B*ut he lisps!"

Retired Admiral Sir Robert Fitch frowned at Priss, the youngest of his five daughters and the only one who had yet to wed. This wasn't the first time they had been through this, and he feared it wouldn't be the last. Still, he pressed on. "What does that have to do with Lakewood's suitability for marriage?"

Priss frowned back at her father, sitting across the long marquetry table from her. She didn't mean to sound like a saucebox, but she had had it up to her ears with his attempts to marry her off. "He calls me *Mith Prith*," she answered crisply. "And I cannot and will not go through life being called *Prith*!"

Father and daughter had met in the library to share a bite of nunch

11

and a bit of conversation. Or so Priss had thought. Now she realized it had merely been an excuse for him to run another one of Henry Oliver's infernal marriage lists by her.

The very thought of Henry Oliver had her casting an exasperated glance at him. Gaudily-tailored as usual and his gray eyes glinting in the shadows, Henry had draped himself ever-so-casually against the mantel of the fireplace at the other end of the room. He responded to her scowl with an impudent smile and a small nod of his head, which served to irritate her even further. Gritting her teeth, she tore her gaze away from him and focused on her father.

Oblivious to the visual exchange between his daughter and his solicitor, the Admiral heaved a sigh and reached for his writing quill. He dipped it into the ink pot and drew a line through Lakewood's name. Then he looked at the next name on the list Henry had compiled.

"Gleason," he read. "The Earl of—"

"A drunkard," she declared.

"A drunkard?" her father repeated with overt disbelief.

"The two times I danced with him in

London, his breath stunk to the stars." Priss shuddered at the memory.

Her father stared at her, his blue eyes troubled. Having achieved honor and renown sailing in the company of the late Admiral Horatio Nelson, he still wore his bushy muttonchops with pride. The thick whiskers made up for the thinning gray hair on his head. Now they fluttered against his cheeks as he blew out a frustrated breath and crossed off Gleason's name.

But his voice filled with renewed enthusiasm when he read the last name on the list. "Dubois. The Marq—"

"He's French," she replied in a dismissive tone.

"Half-French," he shot back.

Priss raised a telltale brow. "And you know what they say about the French."

His reproving expression told her that she'd better have a good explanation.

She did. "Womanizers," she stated emphatically, "every one of them."

His patience worn to a frazzle, her father put down the pen and studied his daughter. She was beautiful, with clear blue eyes fringed by a thick fan of lashes and sun-flushed cheeks. Like her late mother, she was tawny-haired and on the tall, slender side. She would make a stunning bride, he thought, not for the first time, and he had so hoped she would come around to his way of thinking where marriage was concerned. But this was the third time they had been through this exercise, and the third time she had found something wrong with every man he mentioned.

The Admiral cast an inquisitive look at the man who still stood at the far end of the library. He reminded himself to ask Henry about these lists he kept putting together as there seemed to be a distinct divide between quantity and quality. But first . . .

"Congratulations, Priscilla." He returned his attention to his daughter, and his face looked haggard in the late-spring sunlight spilling through the open windows behind him. "You have once again both discarded and denigrated the names of some of the most eligible gentleman in England."

She shot a baleful glance at the man she blamed for this unfortunate situation and then looked back at the man across the table from her and smiled with pride. "Thank you, Father."

"This is nothing to be proud of, young

lady." His eyes, a paler blue than hers, were agleam with aggravation. "You're on the shelf by your own choice at twenty, an age when most young women are either happily married or engaged to be married. And I feel obliged to remind you that the number of suitable men for you to meet is rapidly decreasing by the day."

Knowing she had disappointed him yet again, Priss struck a demure pose, looking down at the hands she had clasped in her lap and saying softly, "I'm sorry, Father."

The Admiral wouldn't have admitted it under penalty of torture, but his last-born was first in his affections. She'd been quite the surprise to her middle-aged parents, drawing moans and groans of embarrassment from their four teenaged daughters and knowing looks from their set of friends when they announced they were once again expecting. Then his beloved wife had died of childbed fever, leaving him bereaved and forced to retire from the Navy to raise their baby daughter on his own.

He'd been gone so often and for such long periods of time during his naval career that he hadn't had much of a hand in the upbringing of Matilda, Drusilla, and twins Bella and Stella. He'd learned just how much he'd missed, however, when baby Priscilla turned her bright blue eyes upon him and gave him her first gummy smile. The nurse he'd hired to help him had dismissed it as gas, but Robert Fitch knew it was love, pure as prayer to a saint. He'd fired the nurse on the spot and taken over Priss's care himself.

When the last of his older daughters married, he sold his London townhouse and moved with Priss to the ruddy cliffs of the Cornish coast. He bought a two-storied mansion built of mellow red brick located two miles from a small but thriving coastal village. The house was roofed with burnt red tiles, crowned by a half-dozen soaring chimneys and flooded with light and sunshine by tall mullioned windows.

Above the main doorway was a massive balcony supported by pillars now clad in green creepers. Unless it was pouring rain or blowing snow, he drank his evening brandy on the balcony, where he had an unobstructed view of the terraces with their connecting steps to the broad and open beach below the house and, beyond, of the deep bay that flowed to and from the sea he so loved.

The Admiral had educated Priscilla. He taught her to read and to write and to study history and maps and the classical languages. When she was old enough, he taught her to swim and to sail and to wield a sword.

He told her stories, too. True stories born of his many and varied naval adventures. His vivid descriptions and enthusiasm brought to life the dramatic chases, near escapes and intense swordplay of life on the sea. Sometimes he told those stories at her bedtime; other times he told them during their after-dinner walks along the beach. But always, unbeknownst to him, they had fueled her dreams and fired her imagination and left her eager for more.

For the finishing touches, he'd hired the former headmistress of a young ladies' academy, who taught Priscilla dancing and deportment and the other social skills required to enter the *beau monde*. Then he'd sent her off to his older daughters, all married and living in London, to oversee her introduction to Society and, he hoped, to the man she would eventually marry.

Priss had soaked up knowledge like a sea sponge and, to her father's delight, had shown a natural aptitude for fencing—so much so that she still practiced it to this day. The sweetest plum in the pudding, however, was her lavish coming-out ball, which had been the talk of the *ton*.

But no sooner had the ball ended, than Priss was ready to pack up and go home to the Cornish coast. Unlike her sisters, who had grown up in London, she wasn't happy there. It was noisy and smelly and crowded with frivolous people who partied half the night and slept half the day.

The strictures of society didn't suit her, either. She couldn't set foot outside of the house without a chaperone, which meant no sailing or fencing, or even exploring the city on her own, for fear of stirring up gossip. And the dirty gray London fog that begrimed people and buildings alike made it difficult at times for her to draw a deep, cleansing breath. She longed to wake up in the sun-splashed mornings at home, to hear the birds singing as they went about their bug-eating or nest-building business, and to smell the crisp tang of salty air that ruffled her hair and bathed her face when she walked on the beach.

She was definitely *not* enamored of any of the witless bucks and would-be gallants who sent her flowers or left their cards or even showed up unexpectedly to call. Some of them were as fussy and frivolous as Henry Oliver. Others sported a rather vacant look in their eyes that hinted at reasoning powers which were less than acute. Still others pressed against her and whispered in her ear, their air of familiarity and fetid breath causing her to turn away in revulsion.

Her sisters begged her to stay, to attend just one more ball, just one more dinner party, to see if there was some man—*any* man at that point—in whom she might be interested. But Priss had made up her mind. She simply couldn't abide another moment of being powdered, painted, perfumed, and paraded around the *ton* dressed up like a stuffed bird, all in a fruitless attempt to attract a suitable bachelor. Finally, her sisters threw up their hands in despair, claiming that no man would ever even want to kiss, much less marry, a hoyden like her.

Ah, if they only knew . . .

What Priss knew was that her destiny did not lie in London. So home to the coast, to her sailing and fencing and refreshing walks on the beach, she went. And at home with her novel-writing and her ailing father she intended to stay.

That worried the Admiral no end. He was nearing seventy and he suffered from several afflictions, not the least of which was a failing heart. His age and his deteriorating physical condition were gall and wormwood to his warrior's spirit. He wasn't afraid to die. He had faced death any number of times upon the distant seas. But he desperately hoped to see Priscilla happily married so he could die in peace, and he had clung on to that hope with the tenacity of a barnacle.

The chances of that happening were looking more remote by the day. Priss was stubborn, and she had turned up her pretty nose every time he so much as mentioned her settling down. Hence, his arrangement with Henry Oliver to make a list of suitable men for her to marry—an arrangement that had yet to produce the desired result.

Now, the Admiral decided it was time to take matters into his own hands.

"Tell me, dear," he encouraged her, "is there any man you *would* like to meet?"

"Yes," Priss said, raising her tawny head to bless him with a smile that showed straight white teeth in the perfect oval of her face.

Her father leaned forward, eager to hear her answer. "And who might that lucky man be?"

"A pirate."


*The Caribbean*


The pirate ship hovered motionlessly, as if biding its time and waiting for the opportune moment to fire upon the merchantman.

Unfortunately for the *James Bond*, its guns were stationary, mechanical monsters locked in place and unable to fire in any direction except straight ahead. That gave the ship of prey, with its light swivel cannons, a distinct advantage in the coming battle.

"Hard to starboard!" the captain ordered.

As the helmsman tilted the *James Bond* into a sharp evasion, Victoria tightened her grip on the railing to keep from being thrown back against the bulwark.

Its sails snapping with the fury of a thunderclap, the pirate ship answered that move by turning at an alarming speed and running parallel to the merchantman.

"All hands! All hands!" the captain shouted.

The crew responded immediately. Some roughly shoved the passengers aside as they rushed to their battle stations. Others began stringing slick, tarred cross-roping down from the shrouds and ratlines

"Best go belowdecks, ladies," the captain urged his female passengers as the brigantine brought its massive battery to bear on his ship.

"Why?" Victoria asked, keeping her eyes on the black-flagged vessel.

"We'll probably be boarded soon, and it's sure to be a bloody process." He gauged the numbers of his fighting force before addressing the male passengers on deck. "You men will stay up here and fight with the crew."

The other women turned to go down to a safer place below, but, for reasons Victoria couldn't explain, the sight of that dark ship exerted a hypnotism like a snake's gaze on her, and she remained at the rail as it swooped in for the kill. The pirate ship was well-armed, with cannons on every deck and what appeared to be hundreds of fighting men gathered in its waist. They stood shoulder to shoulder, motionless and silent, pistols and cutlasses at the ready. Her stomach clenched and clawed as she watched other pirates scramble to their stations and prepare to fire, the barrels of their many guns gleaming in the sun.

Behind her there was a tearing sound that snapped her out of her trance. She turned her head to see sailors slitting open canvas bags with long daggers. Her brows drew together in puzzlement as she watched sand gush from the bags and spill across the deck.

"Why are they doing that?" she asked the portly man who was still standing at the rail.

"You don't want to know," he said tightly.

Victoria whirled and demanded of a bare-chested sailor, "What are you doing?"

"Sanding the decks so we don't slip in the blood when the pirates board us."

## Chapter 3

---

"*A* pirate!" The Admiral echoed in disbelief, the expectant smile perishing on his lips as he stared at Priss in bewilderment.

She held out her hands, palms up, in a plea for his understanding. "I'm writing a new book, you see, and—"

"Hell and damnation, girl!" He pounded his fist on the table with such force that it rattled the dishes that had yet to be cleared. "I don't want to hear another word about those syrupy stories of yours!"

She flashed him a look of injured pride. "My first two romantic novels have sold quite steadily, according to my publisher, and he says the one I'm writing now should do so as well."

Realizing he had insulted his dearly loved daughter, the Admiral sat back in his tall wing chair and took another tack. "I'm sorry, Priss. I love you and I'm truly proud of what you've accomplished with your novels. But there's nothing romantic about pirates. I know because I fought them throughout my naval career."

"I understand that, Father, but—"

"They're blood-thirsty savages," he said dryly.

"The pirate in my story won't be like that," she hurried to explain. "He'll be tall and handsome and—"

"The majority of them are ugly as sin, with patches over their missing eyes, growths and scars on their faces, and half their teeth gone."

"He'll have thick black hair that he ties back with a cord," she went on, "and he'll wear a gold ear—"

"They're thieves and murderers and slave traffickers!" he shot back, irritated by her naiveté. "Women and child abusers, and worse."

But he might as well have been talking to the bookcase-lined walls because she was lost in fleshing out characters and trying out plot points.

"Noble," she murmured, more to herself than to him. "He'll be noble."

Her father shook his head and rolled his eyes heavenward.

"And bold. Oh, he'll be a bold one, he will," she said, warming to her subject now. "A swashbuckling corsair, beholden to none and feared by all who sail the seven seas." She paused a moment to think it through. "But underneath, he'll be a patriot, a man who appears to have abandoned the honest life but is actually in secret service to—"

"A pirate is not a patriot," he finally cut in, his lip curling with contempt at the thought.

"It's fiction, Father," she said with hard-won patience.

"It certainly is," he snapped.

"As such, my pirate can be anyone and do anything I want him to be or do," Priss declared.

"*Your* pirate?" he asked, chafing over her choice of words.

"Yes," she said with authorial pride. "*My* pirate."

His brows drew together until no more than a single deep furrow stood between them. "Where did you get the idea for such a ludicrous story?"

"From you," she said without a moment's hesitation.

That took him aback. "*Me?*"

"Yes," she confirmed, "from all those stories of the sea and of the battles you fought that you used to tell me."

His lips writhed in a smile of weary irony. "Hung from my own yardarm, am I?"

"So it would seem," she agreed cheerfully.

Defeated, he sat back in his chair and sighed.

"Now, Father," she said, "if you will please excuse me . . ."

Anxious to return to her upstairs study to write down her story ideas before they escaped her, she leaped to her feet, lifted the skirt of the blue day dress that she had worn to her fencing exercise that morning, and left the library without so much as a nod in the direction of the garishly-clad man who had borne silent witness to her conversation with her father.

And to think she had once fancied herself in love with that preening rooster!

That preening rooster moved away from the mantelpiece as soon as she closed the double doors behind her and strode forward to consult with his client.

Henry Oliver was seven years older than Priss, but the odd appearance and exaggerated mannerisms he'd adopted in recent years made him appear almost middle-aged. It had puzzled her at first to see that the handsome young man she had known her whole life, the man who had given her her first kiss, the man she had once and quite mistakenly assumed she would marry someday, had changed so utterly and completely.

His hair was powdered with such a heavy hand it was hard to tell just how dark it really was, and the fine particles that had drifted down over his face gave his skin a rather waxen look. The silver-framed lorgnette he used—an eccentric and unnecessary accoutrement, in Priss's opinion—lightened his gray eyes to the color of old, cold ashes. His lips were pinched, his jaw clenched. Beneath a bile green jacket, his stooped shoulders gave him a cave-chested appearance, and the canary yellow ascot and a lacy, bright pink pocket handkerchief were the height of that foppishness Priss so deplored.

There was nothing about him to indicate that he'd been kidnapped and sold on the slave docks as a cabin boy only to be rescued a year later, mottled with bruises and drowning in despair, from the galley of a Spanish pirate ship by the soon-to-retire Admiral Robert Fitch.

Nor would anyone ever have guessed that this frippery fellow whom they assumed would most certainly faint at the first sight of an enemy flag was now living a double life.

Oh, there was much that Henry Oliver kept hidden, the most important being the depth of his feelings for the Admiral's daughter—feelings that he preferred to keep private until he determined the time was right to express them.

That time was coming soon . . .

"Did you hear what she said, Henry?" the Admiral asked him now.

"Yes, sir."

"A pirate." The older man's face reddened with outrage at the thought. "A stealthy rat who would break open our stores, seize our goods and merchandise, and be away with our women on the morning tide while our men are still snoring in their beds."

Henry bit the inside of his cheek to keep himself from smiling at the apt

29

but overstated description. "Indeed."

The Admiral looked at him solemnly. "What would you do, Henry?"

Henry tapped his chin with the lorgnette, his expression growing thoughtful. He pondered the question posed by the man who had tutored him as diligently as he had Priss. That same man had then arranged for him to be educated at Cambridge before he left the only home he remembered to serve King and Country by passing as a dandy who could eavesdrop and pry at all sorts of social occasions without arousing the suspicions of the people he was spying on.

Slowly, the smile that Henry had been withholding appeared. Not the cheeky smile he'd cast at Priss or the bored smirk that he sometimes wore at parties and balls. No, it was a genuine smile, one that relaxed his lips and jaw and brought a secret amusement to his eyes.

"I believe you already know the answer to that, sir," he said.

The two men looked at each other in complete understanding.

After a moment, the Admiral said, "Arrange it, will you, lad?"

"Yes, sir," Henry replied.

"And be sure you introduce the misguided Miss Priss to the ugliest, filthiest, most evil-looking pirate you can find," her father ordered.

## The Caribbean

The *James Bond's* captain paced the deck shouting orders that his crew sprang to obey.

Victoria felt her heart beat frantically in her breast and a chill feeling come upon her as the preparations for battle began taking shape. A bo'sun and his mates staggered under loads of cutlasses and small arms which they stacked in a rack about the mainmast for everyone to employ. The gunner, a jug-eared fellow with some teeth someplace else but not in his mouth, leapt up the companion to the gun-deck. Other men followed hard on his heels.

The captain dispatched one of the bo'sun's mates to prepare another gun for action.

Cannon match and flint in hand, the toothless gunner stood ready to fire when the word was given. The bo'sun's mate also reported himself prepared to receive his orders. Knowing they didn't have powder to waste, the captain bade them to hold their fire for the time being.

Scarcely had he spoken than the pirate craft sent a massive volley of roundshot into the bowels of the merchantman, causing it to sag. The deafening explosion filled Victoria's ears and rocked the deck beneath her feet. She grabbed the rail and clutched it as tightly as she could to keep from falling, just as other swivel guns belched forth chainshot that ripped and tore through the shrouds and sails.

Overhead there was a splintering crash followed by a sough and a thud as the main topmast hurtled to the deck. Victoria covered her head and screwed her eyes shut as shards of wood and other debris struck her. At a piercing scream, she lowered her hands, opened her eyes and watched, horrified, as the sailor who'd been in the crow's nest plunged to his death.

At last, the captain gave the word, shouting savagely, "*FIRE!*"

Shots boomed from the *James Bond.*

The battle was joined!

*Chapter 4*

---

Gone was the powdered hair and face, the telltale lorgnette, and the colorful ascot that Henry Oliver usually wore. In their place a disreputable cap covered tied-back black hair and shaded slate gray eyes. A well-worn seaman's jacket draped his broad shoulders. Nicked and mismatched buttons closed that jacket over a surprisingly muscular chest.

Now he flipped up his collar in hopes of hiding his face before setting out on foot from the apartment above the small law office he kept in the village as much for appearance's sake as for occasional business matters. Although it was late the streets were not entirely deserted. Nighttime meant the muggers and cutthroats would be out in force. Just in case one or more of them was foolish enough to accost him before he reached The Mermaid, he wore a brace of dueling pistols and carried a dagger in his boot.

He tucked his chin into the collar of his coat when he heard a horse's hooves clopping along the cobbled street. Squinting in the darkness, he made out a small cart coming toward him. It was being driven by a man who was singing drunkenly to himself. Moving slowly so as not to draw the inebriated man's attention, he turned around and pressed his nose to the filthy glass window of the local fishmonger's store.

Standing motionless, Henry heard the cart slow. He felt rather than saw the other man taking a long look at him. The harbor was fog-bound tonight, and the shore lights were barely visible against the darkened sky, both of which he hoped would decrease the chance of him being recognized. Still, one could never be too careful in an otherwise proper English village that just happened to have a port that was frequented by pirates and smugglers.

Finally the man clicked his tongue at the horse, and the clip-clop of its hooves faded into the distance. Henry waited a moment to be sure it was safe before he turned and resumed his trek to The Mermaid.

Ships' bells tolled the hour, and the air held the dank smell of the sea. Henry hated the sea and all its memories of being beaten and whipped and kicked around by the Spanish pirate who had purchased him from the slave market, of staring despondently at the far-off horizon through blackened eyes, of hanging his aching head in misery knowing that death was his only hope for escape. Whips and chains, loneliness and pain, that was the sea.

And here was The Mermaid.

He had to duck to avoid striking his head against the age-darkened lintel. Stinking of tobacco smoke, alcohol, and body odor, and lit by the dim flicker of a few sputtering candles that were set here and there on random tables, The Mermaid was one of the most notorious smugglers inns in this part of Cornwall. It was also the perfect place for sailors and pirates alike to gather gossip, hire a cutpurse or a murderer, and make traitorous plans.

The sounds of arguing, belching, and cursing were as thick, garbled, and unpleasant as the smells. Looking around, Henry wondered if they had opened the filthy windows or mopped the sticky floor in the last ten years. Probably not, he decided.

He finally saw the man he had come to meet. As hideous looking as ever, he was sitting at a small round table across the room with a pint of ale in front of him. Henry passed a raggedly-dressed fellow holding a dirty pipe to his mouth as well as a drunk who was sleeping with his head in a plate of half-eaten, greasy-looking stew as he made his way through the crowd.

Odd the Vonck was the ugliest pirate he'd ever encountered. Scattered strings of oily, mud-brown hair clung like wet seaweed around his scarred and beard-stubbled face. His left eye was missing but he refused to wear a patch, finding untoward amusement in the shocked reactions of women and children to the empty socket. His mashed-in nose looked as if it would fly off his face if he sneezed, and his oft-broken jaw lurched to the left.

Tonight he was a flamboyantly shabby sight, dressed in a faded blue silk waistcoat with torn and filthy lace at the cuffs and a tricorne hat with a crippled plume. A thumbnail-sized emerald sparkled in his right ear. The jewel helped draw people's attention away from the spiky tuft of hair sticking out of his left ear. A brace of pistols was belted at his waist along with two knives, their handles polished smooth from use.

Henry and Vonck had served under the same ruthless Spaniard at the same time, and Henry had heard from reliable sources that Vonck and his recently-acquired ship were for hire. The brigand was ripe for any venture, it was said, from scuttling the French to attacking merchant vessels to raiding seaside villages. His was a stomach that refused nothing so long as there was money to be had.

And money, Henry had. He had deliberately waited the week it took Vonck to finish caulking his ship to send him a message to meet here tonight. Now it was time to see if he was game for helping to pull off the Admiral's ruse.

The fact that Henry had his own personal reasons for wanting things to go as planned was nobody else's business.

The sea-going bandit opened a gap-toothed smile as Henry approached. It was a gruesome spectacle to behold.

"Damme if ye're not a sight for a sore eye, boy-o."

Laughing, Henry took the stool across from him and crossed his arms on the table scarred with ancient stains and dagger cuts. "I take it you were surprised to receive a message from me."

"Aye." Frowning now, Vonck fingered the roaring dragon handle of his pewter tankard. "We gave ye up for dead after th' Brits boarded Dos Sebastián's ship."

"Why is that?"

"We figured they threw all ye scabby slaves in the drink."

Henry's mouth twisted wryly. "Yet here I am, big as life."

Vonck lifted his tankard in a salute. "That ye are."

Now Henry tipped his head. "And you, as well."

The old sea dog screwed his face into a sneer. "No thanks t' that Admiral Whats'isname."

"Fitch," Henry supplied. "Admiral Robert Fitch."

"Aye." Vonck almost shouted in his anger. "And a reg'lar Jack Ketch, he were, makin' me ol' mates dance the hempen jig."

"Piracy is a hanging offense," Henry reminded him.

Vonck's lip curled with derision. "They was entitled t' a trial."

"They received one aboard ship," Henry replied in an even tone.

"With that Admiral playin' judge and jury."

"As maritime law permits."

A buxom young barmaid carrying dirty dishes in one hand and empty mugs in the other approached their table.

Vonck held Henry's gaze for a moment and then he shrugged and took a swallow of ale. "Will ye have a pint with me?"

"I'll have a brandy," Henry said to the barmaid. "And another pint for my associate."

As she nodded and made to leave with their order, a pair of grimy hands from a passerby reached out and closed around her waist. Keeping the dishes and mugs she carried well in hand, she kneed her molester where it would hurt him most and left him screaming in agony as he staggered away. Crude laughter and rude comments from the pirates at the next table over trailed her as she made her way to the bar.

"So how did you escape?" Henry asked his companion as the laughter died down.

"A number o' us, includin' the Spaniard, managed t' slip over the side and into a jolly boat afore the shackles went on," Vonck explained. "The rest o' the lads were tossed in the 'old and chained down like a pack o' wild dogs."

Henry considered this for a moment and then said, with a frown, "Dos Sebastián always was a sly one."

"Cunning as twenty devils," Vonck the pirate agreed.

"What's he up to now?" Henry figured he might as well gather any information that might prove useful to the man who would soon be taking his place in the service.

Vonck shrugged. "Th' usual."

"Thieving upon the seas and scuttling ships?" Henry prompted.

The pirate nodded before adding, "And tradin' in slaves."

Henry sat back in surprise, "That's a new wrinkle."

"A fruitful one, too. Sellin' slaves made 'im rich enough to buy a new ship."

"A new ship, 'eh?"

"Sleek as a London lady," the pirate

said, "and armed as 'eavily as a small fort."

Henry pursed his lips. "What flag is he flying?"

"A hawk. Calls hisself the Hawk of the Sea." Vonck gulped down the last of his pint and shot him a sharp glance with his one eye. "Why d'ye ask?"

"Mere curiosity." Realizing he'd asked enough questions for one sitting, Henry tucked away the information to pass along at a later date and then gave the scurrilous lout sitting across the table from him a crooked smile. "I understand you have your own ship, as well."

"The Sea Devil." The pirate's chest puffed up and he looked as proud as a new papa. "Captured 'er in th' Caribe. She's a beauty, too, now that we scraped th' barnacles and seaweed off 'er bottom and patched and painted 'er up."

The barmaid set down their drinks and Henry gave her a gold coin that left her pop-eyed.

There was more, much more, where that came from. He had blunt enough to buy Vonck's services ready to his hand. It came from the Admiral, of course, and had been given to him to set up the ruse intended to disabuse a certain stubborn miss of the preposterous notion that pirates were an attractive lot.

The Admiral had laid down the law about how it was to be carried out. Not so much as a hair on Priscilla's head was to be harmed—a cat-o-nine-tails, or worse, awaited anyone who so much as touched her. What she needed was simply a good scare. An encounter on the beach with the likes of a pirate as repulsive as Odd the Vonck should give her precisely that.

It might also give Henry a long-awaited chance to redeem himself in her eyes. Or so he hoped.

The two men drank in silence for a few minutes while Henry mulled over the best way to broach his business with Vonck.

Finally, the crafty pirate, seeming to read Henry's hesitation and anxious to conquer it for the sake of such profit as he conceived might lie in the proposal that he scented, paved the way for him.

He leaned forward conspiratorially and asked in a low voice, "Am I right in thinkin' that ye have some sort o' matter t' propose t' me?"

"That you are," Henry confirmed.

"Out with it then, for there never was a man more ready t' serve ye," Vonck assured him.

Lowering his own voice so as not to be overheard by the loud-mouthed pirates at the next table, Henry got down to business. "I have a job for you."

"Speak up, boy-o," Vonck said, turning his hair-tufted ear toward Henry. "I'm near deef from cannon fire."

"I said I have a job for you," Henry all but shouted.

Vonck's eye lit up at the news and his few remaining teeth, yellowed and chipped and widely spaced, shown in his mouth when he opened it in glee. He sat back, slurped down another slug of ale from his fresh tankard, and then wiped his hair-prickled chin with the back of his hand.

He leaned forward again and, fingering the emerald in his other ear, he asked, "What sort'a job ye be talkin' about?"

Henry leaned forward as well and proceeded to give the old pirate a brief outline of the scheme the Admiral had approved. "Her father will say he doesn't feel well, so he'll ask me to walk on the beach with her. Shortly after we begin walking is when you'll come upon us. Once she gets a good look at you—"

"He'd trust me near his daughter?" Vonck asked in a skeptical tone.

Henry's eyes turned stone cold. "Like I said, I'll be with her. And," he added in a threatening tone, "I'll be armed."

Vonck looked horror-stricken. "I don't want ye shooting me!"

"As long as you do what I say, I won't have to," Henry warned him.

The pirate gave it brief consideration. "That big bay has a little neck, as I r'member."

"Go in before sunset and drop anchor like you're spending the night in the cove."

"We'll be seen from the village," Vonck pointed out.

"Lower your flag and furl your sails and people will think you're dredging for oysters."

The pirate drained his tankard and slammed it down on the table. "Ye said the Admiral'd be willin' t' pay."

Henry nodded and started the negotiations. "One hundred pounds."

"Three 'undred," the scalawag countered.

Henry shook his head.

"Two-fifty?"

Henry raised an eyebrow.

Vonck sighed. "Two 'undred."

Since that was the amount the Admiral had set as a limit, Henry agreed to the two hundred pounds.

"'Alf now an' 'alf when the deed is done," Vonck demanded.

Henry had come prepared for that as well. Surreptitiously, he drew a purse from his pocket and passed it under the table. Without so much as looking into its contents, the pirate snatched it from his hand and put it in his jacket pocket.

"Now t' the ways and means," Vonck said.

Speaking no louder than necessary so the partially deaf pirate could hear him, Henry told Vonck exactly what he wanted him to do and when he wanted him to do it.

Neither of them noticed was that one of the big-eared pirates sitting at the next table had not only watched the money change hands but he had also scooted his stool close enough to overhear every word that was said.

Victoria watched in horrified astonishment as the blast from the merchantman went sailing over the forecastle of the pirate ship. The merchantman's captain cursed his gunner for having aimed too high and signaled to the bo'sun's mate to fire his gun at the enemy amidships.

But even as he signaled there was a flash of color and light from the pirate ship followed by an ear-splitting roar. Red-hot pieces of metal whistled by. Debris flew everywhere. The merchantman's sails caught fire and its sand-covered deck was suddenly smothered in thick, eye-stinging smoke.

Victoria lost her grip on the rail and staggered backward when the bone-jarring barrage hit them.

The portly man standing next to her grabbed hold of her arm to keep her from falling. "You'd best go below now."

"Yes," she belatedly agreed.

But before she could regain her footing and make to do so, the pirate ship veered yet again and rammed the *James Bond* so hard that she and the man were flung in opposite directions.

Victoria landed half way across the deck and laid there for a moment, stunned, as barrels tore loose from their lashings and rolled, spilling the rum and oil and sugar that had been purchased in the islands to mix with the sand. Rigging split and came snaking down. Sailors toppled over the torn and twisted rails and tumbled head over heels into the killing sea as the merchantman listed even more ominously.

Undaunted by the bone-crushing, timber-shattering collision, the dark ship peeled away, only to come abreast of the merchantman. When they were within a dozen yards of each other, the pirate ship launched its grappling irons across the gap. The metal teeth made a terrible grinding sound as they bit into the rails and pulled the two ships together.

Pirates firing pistols and brandishing swords swarmed like ravaging locusts onto the deck of the crippled craft by way of a hastily erected, steeply canted bridge of long, wide planks. The clang of steel on steel filled the air. Men yelled and cursed. From belowdecks came the screams of terrified women and children.

Victoria clutched a rope that was hanging loose and pulled herself up off the deck. No sooner had she gained her feet than the rope broke and she was left holding a useless piece of hemp. The ship pitched again and she swayed, drunk from weariness, fear, and shock. Then she fell to her knees only to feel cold water soak through her skirt to her skin.

The chill sobered her. She pushed to a standing position once more and saw a hefty brigand, his violent red hair standing upright in sweaty spikes, racing straight toward her.

*Chapter 5*

---

"We've an hour to dinner, Miss, if you'd like to have a bath first."

A startled Priss looked up and saw Alice Lee, her pretty, apple-cheeked maid, standing in the doorway of her study. She'd been so engrossed in the boarding of the *James Bond* that she had completely lost track of time. Now her hair was tousled, her dress was wrinkled, and her fingers were stained with ink.

"Yes, thank you, Alice, a bath sounds wonderful." She set her pen aside, closed the ink pot, and then opened her desk drawer to put away today's pages. Her neck was stiff from leaning over her manuscript for so long and she tipped her head from side to side, trying to work the knots out of it. A warm bath to ease the ache in her shoulders and back sounded heavenly. "I'll be along in a minute."

"Yes, Miss." Alice nodded and left to fill the tub.

Priss closed the desk drawer and sighed with contentment. Her study opened off her bedroom and was her refuge, a wonderfully inviting room where she could let her imagination run as free as the warm breeze that wafted in through the open window. A delicately-carved mahogany desk that had belonged to her mother faced the door, and a beautiful Turkey design carpet—a gift from her father—graced the floor.

There was a small hearth on one side of the room along with a comfortable chair and footrest. After dark of a winter's eve she could usually be found in her wool wrapper and slippers curled up in front of a toasty fire, a candle providing proper lighting as she read one of the hundreds of books from the shelves that lined the walls of the library downstairs.

Her bedroom was decorated in shades of blue and green, which gave everything the appearance of being underwater. A carpet similar in design to the one in the study covered the floor. Two windows draped in silk flanked a large four-poster bed that wore a light moiré quilt. A massive wardrobe handed down through her father's family stood against one wall, and a Japanese lacquered screen featuring airy chimeras and blossoms against another. The hearth promised warmth in winter and was filled with fresh flowers in spring and summer. Today a vase of freshly-picked sea pinks made a pretty splash against the brick.

The screen had been moved aside to reveal a small porcelain tub on cloven hooves. A few feet away, a rosewood stool sat before a matching dressing table with a beveled looking glass atop it. Alice kept up a lively chatter while Priss undressed and stepped into the tub from which tempting tendrils of steam arose. She gave a blissful sigh as she slid deeper into the warm water and felt the kinks float out of her body. Alice picked up the discarded clothes and set a length of toweling and clean undergarments on the stool so they would be near at hand when Priss got out of the tub.

"Feel good, Miss?" she asked as she lifted a bottle of lotion from atop the dressing table.

"Like heaven." Priss had washed but was so comfortable she allowed herself to relax a few minutes more before getting out.

"How goes your story?" Alice inquired.

"Very well, thank you."

Alice wrested the doors of the wardrobe open so Priss could select a dinner dress from the brightly colored assortment hanging there and then turned back toward the bathtub. "I didn't mean to eavesdrop, Miss, truly I didn't . . ."

"But?" Priss prompted when Alice's voice faded.

"I heard you tell your father a week past that you were writing a story about a pirate."

"That I am."

"A *handsome* pirate," Alice repeated coquettishly.

Priss's laughter bubbled forth. "A handsome and *noble* pirate."

Alice's brown eyes twinkled in anticipation as she came back to help her mistress out of the tub. "Oh, I can't wait to hear it!"

"*Hear* it?" Priss rose and let the maid wrap the towel around her before she stepped out of the tub and onto a small, soft rug laid on the floor beside it.

"Yes, Miss."

"Why not read it?"

Alice shrugged. "Because I can't read."

Priss was aghast. "You can't read?"

"Nor write."

"Whyever not?"

"I never had the schooling." There wasn't a speck of self-pity in Alice's tone. Rather it was as brisk as the motions she used to rub her mistress dry.

"Oh, Alice, I'm so—"

"It's all right, Miss," Alice assured her as she slathered rose-scented lotion on her skin. "My sister works for a lady who taught *her* to read so she—"

"I could teach you to read," Priss offered.

Alice dismissed the proffer with a wave of her hand. "Oh, you're too busy, what with your writing and fencing and looking for a husband."

"Looking—I'm *not* looking for a husband!" Priss said, vexed.

"As you say, Miss." Alice's face flushed and her chin dipped.

53

Priss had the grace to apologize. "I'm sorry, Alice."

"You've had a long day," Alice said by way of forgiveness.

"I know Father wants me to marry—"

"As most fathers do," Alice said in a practical vein.

Priss made a moue. "Mine especially."

"And most daughters usually want to marry," her maid pointed out as she wiped the lotion residue off her hands onto the damp toweling.

"Yes, of course, but . . ." Priss sighed. How to explain that she'd rather remain a spinster than marry a man whose name had been plucked off a list created by the very man she'd resigned herself to living without? Or that she'd recently fallen victim to her own romantic fantasies and was half in love with a fictional pirate against whom all other men seemed to pale? She couldn't, not without sounding like a complete ninnyhammer, so she left well enough alone.

Alice helped Priss into her undergarments and then bade her sit down at the dressing table so she could fix her hair. "Cook said Mr. Oliver is coming to dinner tonight."

The news ruined Priss's relaxed mood. "I hope he's not bringing another one of his lists."

"Wherever does he get the names of those awful men, anyway?" Alice asked.

Priss had often wondered the same thing. "That's a good question. I'll have father ask him first chance."

Alice pinned up Priss's hair before threading a thin blue ribbon through the tawny waves and then leaving a few wisps free to curl at her forehead and along the nape of her neck. Satisfied with her handiwork, Alice put the comb and brush away and returned to the open wardrobe.

"Mr. Oliver certainly wears his shirt points on the high side, doesn't he?" she said.

"I'm surprised he doesn't cut a cheek on them," Priss said dryly.

Alice giggled as she sorted through the multitude of dresses in the wardrobe, smoothing their skirts and sleeves as she went. "Still, he always treats me with respect. He bobs his head and asks me how I am. And he's just as polite to Will and Cook and the rest of us, too."

"That's as it should be." Despite

her heartfelt declaration, Priss was ashamed to admit that she'd never even noticed how Henry treated the servants.

Alice turned back toward the dressing table; her brow furrowed as if she had just remembered something else she wanted to say. "And speaking of Mr. Oliver, Miss . . ."

"Yes?"

"I heard the strangest thing about him from Bert."

Given that it was Henry they were talking about, Priss couldn't say she was surprised. "From Bert the groom?"

Alice nodded. "He goes into the village on his night off, you know."

"No," Priss admitted, "I didn't know."

"Gets half-foxed, he does," Alice said in a disapproving tone.

Priss sat back in surprise. "*Bert*?"

"Yes, Miss," Alice confirmed. "He told me he was driving his cart back from the village a few nights ago when he saw a man he said looked like Mr. Oliver approaching The Mermaid."

"The Mermaid!" Priss had never been inside the smugglers inn, but she had heard any number of stories about it—none of them good.

"Dressed like a common tar, he was, Bert said."

"*Henry*?" Priss said with incredulity.

Alice gave an even more vigorous nod. "Bert said Mr. Oliver was wearing a cap and a seaman's coat and carrying what looked to be a pistol in the waistband of his breeches. He turned his head away and looked through the fishmonger's window, but Bert recognized his reflection in the glass."

Priss's first inclination was to dismiss it as a case of mistaken identity, especially since the groomsman had been tippling. Then she wondered if Henry might have a long-lost brother or cousin who resembled him. After all, he'd been shanghaied as a young boy and then sold into slavery shortly after, and he'd always claimed he didn't remember much about his family.

Realizing she was letting her imagination run away with her, Priss shook her head. "Now why would a pompous fop like Henry Oliver frequent a squalid place like The Mermaid?"

The question seemed to flummox the gossipy Alice. She gave another shrug and turned her attention back to the wardrobe. "Which gown do you wish to wear this evening?"

"The blue lawn."

"Oh, I like that one, Miss."

"And I'll need my white silk shawl."

Alice smiled. "You'll be taking a walk on the beach this evening?"

"A *long* walk," Priss confirmed, planning to excuse herself as soon as possible and escape the dining room before her father could present her with another one of Henry's lists of potential suitors.


*The Caribbean*

Victoria leaped to one side as the red-haired brigand lunged for her.

She whirled, intending to flee, but her skirt, heavy with sea water and bloody sand, twined about her legs and the disgusting pudding covering the deck sucked her slippers off her feet. Together, they slowed her down to the point that the pirate was able to catch her about the waist. He dragged her backwards, twisting and kicking and screaming, toward what remained of the side rail.

Suddenly she was free. She stumbled, regained her balance, and spun on stockinged feet to see her captor had come to a stop, his eyes and mouth opened wide with surprise. Then he fell, landing face down on the deck not too far from the mortally wounded captain.

Looking up, she saw the portly man who'd told her to go below holding a cutlass that he'd smacked flat against the back of the brigand's head. She clapped a hand across her mouth in shock when a shot that narrowly missed her hit him in the chest, spattering her face, the back of her hand, and her torn sleeve with his blood as he dropped in a neatly-dressed bundle.

The battle was lost, Victoria realized, looking around her with utter despair.

The *James Bond* was riding low in the water, listing to port. Smoke from the flames devouring the sails and everything else in sight burned her eyes, and the metallic scent of spent gunpowder stung her nose. Strangled gurgles in the wood, terrifying sea dirges, told her it was only a matter of time before the merchantman sank. The captain as well as a majority of sailors and male passengers had died defending the ship. The few who'd survived were being frog-marched to the pirate ship.

Screams and sobs emanated from belowdecks. Some of the pirates had teamed up to lug a dozen or more huge wooden chests toward the rail. Others carried the terrified women and a handful of crying children over their scarred and sweating shoulders to the pirate ship, to be held for ransom . . . or worse.

The thought of that filled her with fear and anger. Pushing her half-loosened hair out of her smoke-blurred eyes, Victoria picked up the cutlass. She had never willingly harmed anyone or anything in her life, not even the flies or the lizards or the blood-sucking mosquitoes that were part of everyday life in Martinique. But something in her had snapped. Holding the heavy weapon with both hands, she vowed she would not be taken alive, that no pirate—

And then, through the pall of smoke and flame, she saw him.

He was coming for her . . .

## Chapter 6

———— ∾ ————

"I wonder where Henry is," the Admiral fretted as he spooned up the last strawberry and the last bit of sherry in his fruit cup.

"He *is* a man of business," Priss reminded him, "so perhaps a matter of business delayed him."

She hadn't missed seeing Henry at the table this evening, but she dared not tell her father that. He'd never made a secret of the fact that he regarded Henry as the son he'd never had and he took a great deal of pleasure in his company.

That didn't hurt Priss's feelings or make her jealous. Henry had been a part of her life for as long as she could remember. She understood that his seaborne rescue had created a strong bond between the two men. And she honestly believed that the time they spent together, either closeted in the library after one of Henry's long absences or sitting on the terrace sharing a brandy while discussing the day's issues kept her father young at heart.

But it was Henry's mysterious absences, sometimes a month or more long, coupled with the fact that he now looked like a complete stranger, that had sparked Priss's curiosity and imagination. Where did he go? And why? Had he simply turned into a vacuous social butterfly, invited to all the right house parties and weekend hunts in all the right places?

Or was there a more sinister explanation for his recent appearance and those odd intervals in which he seemed to drop out of sight? Was he a thief who'd mastered the art of disguise? Or, more intriguing yet, was he a spy?

The questions jostled and pushed against each other in her mind. She couldn't ask him, of course, so she did what she did best. She fashioned a hero and a heroine, plotted a story built around her questions and her father's stories of the sea, and set about writing a new book.

Writing gave Priss a sense of purpose and brought a welcome structure to her days. An early riser, she ate a light breakfast of toast with marmalade and unsweetened tea, after which she walked the beach or practiced her fencing for an hour before sitting down in her study to write. Sometimes the words flowed like wine onto the page. Other times, she stared into space wondering what should happen next. Yet somehow, by the time she joined her father and, oftentimes, Henry for dinner, she found that she had written at least a handful of pages.

But since his latest return from who-knew-where, Henry had shown a disturbing ability to throw her off balance. She'd catch him staring at her from across the table or from the far end of a room. His glimmering gray eyes would meet hers, kindling the memory of the passionate kiss and impassioned embrace she'd never forget. Her heart would lurch into a wild dance of jubilation at the recollection, and she would find herself leaning toward him as if to remind him of their shared experience.

Then the light in his eyes would dim and he would turn to speak to her father, or if there were other people in the room, make a flippant remark to one of them, and she'd be left with a sinking heart trying to sort through the upheaval in her emotions. That was the main reason she had decided to avoid him as much as she could. Better to spend her time writing or reading or walking on the beach than let him continue to unsettle her so.

Besides, she was too engrossed in writing her new novel to worry about whatever was alight beneath the tempting tilt of Henry's powdered brows. Her father's dismissal aside, she knew her readers. And because she had loved and lost, she was able to pour both passion and poignancy onto every page. She wrote about heroes who swept heroines off their feet, sent their hearts racing and setting their blood afire. Heroes who saved heroines from dastardly villains or even at times from their own foolish behavior. Her first book sold slowly but regularly. When the second came out the following year, it sold better, and her publisher reissued her first. Now she was eager to complete her third book because she believed it would be her best seller yet.

Priss felt content. She lived with her

father whom she dearly loved, and she had a career that she also loved. More important than the monetary reward that came her way was the freedom to pursue her interests. If she was having a rough go with a scene, she could turn her attention to practicing her fencing or to walking on the beach. Doubts did occasionally assail her as she lay alone at night in her four-poster bed. When they did she was forced to admit that passion on the page was a poor substitute for the real thing.

Her father reached into the pocket of his brocade vest and pulled out his watch. His veined hands trembled as he pried it open to check it for at least the tenth time since he'd come to the table. The unease that had plagued him all day returned in full force on seeing it was going on six-thirty.

"I told him we were eating at six o'clock," he said.

"As we always do." Priss had long ago selected that time in deference to her father's age as well as his penchant for retiring at an early hour.

Frowning, he closed the watch and tucked it back in his pocket. "And he promised he would be here at five-thirty sharp."

"I'm sure it was something out of his control that kept him away," she said to soothe him, wondering why Henry's failure to arrive for dinner had so agitated him. "After all, he likes the meals Cook prepares."

As did they all. Thanks to their proximity to port and to the vendors who hawked their wares there, Cook routinely served freshly caught fish or even oysters from the bay along with other delicious, nutritious and sometimes exotic dishes. Tonight they had eaten sea bass sautéed in olive oil and a knob of butter and served with lemon wedges. There had also been a small pie of macaroni mixed with chopped tomatoes, and, for dessert, cups of fresh fruit sprinkled with sherry. A dry white wine had complemented the repast.

Now that they were finished, it was time for her father to take his evening brandy.

Priss touched her linen napkin to her lips and then laid it beside her plate. The terrace doors were open, admitting a lovely breeze laden with the sweet smell of the profusely blooming roses. The westerly sun glinted off the gold utensils and created multi-colored rainbows where the beams hit the crystal glasses. Raising her index finger, she signaled the footman standing nearby to begin removing the dishes and serving platters.

"Including Mr. Oliver's setting, Miss?" he asked.

"Yes, thank you, Will."

"I'll take my brandy on the balcony," her father said, rising gingerly from his chair.

Feeling a bit dizzy, he stood for a moment with his legs braced apart as if balancing himself against heavily rolling seas. When the spell finally passed, he started making his way out of the dining room. But he could still feel he was walking a tad unsteadily as he headed toward the central staircase.

Priss rose as well, gathered her light silk shawl around her shoulders, and rushed to slip her arm through his. She'd been trying to convince him to use a walking stick so he wouldn't fall. Yet so far the elaborately-carved walnut stick with the gold tip that she had commissioned for his last birthday remained unused in the copper stand by the front door.

"I think I'll take a walk on the beach

while you enjoy your brandy," she said by way of making conversation.

He stopped halfway up the stairs and eyed her with an expression of alarm. "No."

She stopped, too, and looked at him in surprise. "I beg your pardon?"

"You heard me," he said on a rasp of breath, and resumed climbing up to the second floor. "You're not to walk on the beach by yourself."

"But I do so all the time," she reminded him in a calm tone.

"If you want to walk on the beach tonight, you'll have to wait for Henry," he countered, his voice emphatic.

Priss could hardly believe her ears. "Henry? Why should I wait for Henry?"

"Because I said so." With that, he shook off her arm and stepped through the open doorway onto to the balcony.

The evening had retained the day's warmth, which would provide welcome relief to his gout-ridden limbs. Roses blooming in large pots on either side of the doors perfumed the air. The sun continued its lazy journey toward the horizon and already the few puffs of cloud overhead were turning a vibrant pink in anticipation of a glorious sunset.

The Admiral lowered his still-trim frame into an iron chair with a pillowed seat. The way the chair was angled on the terrace, he could look out upon the bay and find a measure of solace in its sparkling water. A small tiled table that he'd picked up in Portugal following the Battle of Cape St. Vincent sat to his right, and it was there that Will set the brandy glass. Waving his hand to dismiss the footman, he lifted the glass to his lips and took a sip.

Priss sank to the chair on the other side of the table, thinking there was something truly odd about her father's manner this evening. Perhaps his health was failing faster than she knew. Maybe he wanted Henry here when he told her the end was near. Blinking back tears at the thought, she studied him covertly, noting that the lines on his forehead were deeper, his cheekbones sharper. His breath was sometimes labored these days, and though weary, his eyes were as observant as ever.

Reaching over, she laid a loving hand on his arm. "Are you feeling unwell, Father?"

His fierce countenance softened. "No worse than usual."

If it wasn't his health . . . she thought

about the way he'd kept checking the time throughout dinner. And the brusque way he'd denied her permission to walk on the beach. Both were so unlike him they triggered a suspicion in her mind.

"Is there something you're not telling me?" she asked him.

He gave her a sidelong glance. "Such as?"

"I don't know," she said, attempting to mask her frustration. "Have you heard a rumor or seen a sign of—" It struck her then like a blow. "Are you in danger?"

"No, no, my girl." Her father patted her hand, then turned his attention back to the water, dappled now with copper and crimson shadows.

Priss followed his gaze with her own, wondering what it was that held him fast. From their watcher's eyrie she could see a ship lying at anchor on the left bank of the bay. Its sails were furled, and a flock of seagulls circled above it, their noisy and insolent cries carrying across the water in the still spring air.

A second ship left a long ripple in the water as it dropped anchor across the bay, on the right bank and slightly behind the first ship. Several men scrambled down the rope ladder hung over the side, climbed into a jolly boat and began rowing the small craft towards the beach.

It wasn't that unusual to see ships this close to shore. Some of them used the bay as a haven in a storm, others dredged for oysters in the shallow, salty waters near the shore. Still others anchored in the cove and sent a crew to purchase a fresh stock of provisions in the nearby village, as the one that had launched the jolly boat appeared to be doing.

What *was* unusual was that neither vessel was flying a flag.

The flagless ships bobbing placidly in the water like painted toys sparked a memory in the back of the Admiral's mind of an incident during the Battle of Martinique, when a French brig tried to decoy the ships under his command by maneuvering so as to tempt them toward a shoal lying off a nearby island. He'd suspected a ruse and, instead of falling into the trap, had turned and offered battle. That decisive action had not only brought him victory but it had also saved his life and the lives of the men under his command.

Now, he felt a shark bite of remorse at the thought of his own imprudent scheme. He had enlisted Henry's help in order to show Priss how wrong she was about the ways and means of pirates. It had seemed the right thing to do at the time, another lesson she needed to learn, and he'd meant no harm to her or to anyone else. Yet as much as it pained him to admit it, he was in the wrong—that what he had put in motion may instead have put her in grave danger.

Despair settled down upon him. He had no way of contacting Henry at the moment, and time was of desperate value. Somehow, some way, he needed to call a halt to this reckless ruse before it was too late.

But it wasn't too late, he reminded himself. He could still turn this ship around. He could still set things right, and he would. Tomorrow he would confess all to Priss and beg her forgiveness. Tonight, however, he would do what he had to do to keep her safe, even if meant sounding like an irrational ogre in the process.

He took a sip of brandy and then drew a determined breath. "It isn't safe nor is it seemly for a young woman to be walking the beach when strange ships are anchored in the bay."

The peculiar way he said it drew Priss's attention to him. His jaw was squared, his mouth a grim line. There was something amiss here, something she didn't yet fathom.

"But you just said Henry could walk with me," she countered.

"I've changed my mind," he said. "You'll stay off the beach tonight, with or without Henry."

His voice had the ring of a royal decree. Priss opened her mouth to protest, but he silenced her with a wave of his hand. "I'm too tired to argue. I'm going to bed."

"Shall I wake you when Henry comes?" she asked, her confusion turning to concern.

He tossed back the rest of his brandy, set the empty glass on the side table, and then rose slowly to his feet. "If I'm asleep when he arrives, tell him I said it's off."

"Off?" She gave him a puzzled look. "What—"

"I'll explain tomorrow," he promised before turning and tottering into the house, leaving her sitting alone and agape on the balcony.

Priss glanced at the jolly boat, moving steadily toward the beach, and then back at the doorway through which her father had just made his exit. She rarely disagreed with him, and she couldn't remember the last time she'd disobeyed him. But his curt order that she stay off the beach tonight coupled with his inexplicable behavior had triggered her curiosity.

What could it hurt for her to slip down the terrace steps? It wouldn't be too serious a breach of parental authority if she didn't have to set foot on the sand. She could stand on the bottom step and look up and down the beach. Maybe then she could figure out why her father was so determined she stay put.

Drawing her shawl about her shoulders, Priss stood and left the balcony.

*The Caribbean*

Tall and broad-shouldered, the approaching pirate wore a bloodstained white shirt with an open neck and full sleeves, close-fitting black breeches, and three-quarter boots. A red bandana was tied around his dark hair and a gold earring adorned his left ear. A pair of primed pistols with elaborately carved handles hung from his belt as did a leather knife sheath from which a silver handle cast a wicked glitter.

Spellbound, Victoria watched him move toward her. He walked with the grace of a panther on the prowl, the purpose of a man on a mission. Nothing deterred him, not even the remnant of a burning timber that fell between them and sent sparks flying. He kicked it aside and kept his gaze focused on her.

With a sickening clarity that nearly choked off her breath, she knew that he meant to take her. He smiled, his teeth flashing whitely in his soot- and sun-darkened face when she tightened her grip on the cutlass and raised it in a threatening pose. Her hands and arms shook from the weight, but she held it as if her life depended on it, prepared to defend herself to the death.

And still he smiled.

Still he came . . .

He stopped an arm's reach from her, and she could see him up close. His eyes were a deep winter-gray and hawklike, missing nothing. He gazed at her intently. Her dirty and disheveled appearance aside, she sensed that he found no flaw in what he saw. He propped his hands on his narrow hips, as if waiting for her to make the first move.

She poked the sharp point of the cutlass against his midsection, not forceful enough to tear his shirt or to draw blood but more of a warning jab. Solid, a wall of muscle, it didn't give. He stared at her for a long moment, then reached over and eased the cutlass from her locked fingers.

The ship listed even more ominously, and Victoria realized she was beaten, a bleak resignation that left her as weak as the water now gushing onto the deck. Then her mind went blank and her knees buckled.

He dropped the cutlass and caught her before she fell, hefting her slender body across his shoulder. Victoria knew soft blackness and jolting as he carried her away from the smoking, sinking devastation of the merchantman. Another jolt as he leapt onto the deck of the pirate ship.

And then nothing.

# Chapter 7

———✺———

*P*riss stole out the front door and closed it softly behind her.

Her father had spared no expense, bringing the best horticulturists and masons from London to restore order and beauty to the tangled wilderness that had surrounded the house when he bought it lo those many years ago. Now the gardens on either side of the kidney-stoned front walk were in full fragrant bloom, and the matching marble statues of nymphs and imps that stood in the middle of each gleamed in white brilliance against the dusky sky. Straight ahead, bordered by granite balustrades on one side and Cornish palms skirted with heather on the other, were the three reconstructed terraces with their connecting flights of steps that led to the beach.

The incessant churring of a night-jar perched in one of the palms echoed the beat of Priss's heart as she hurried along the walk. The warm breeze tossed the soft curls surrounding her face and at her nape and teased the edge of her shawl and the skirt of her dress. The first star, a mere twinkle, appeared in the dimming sky above her.

She tried to sort out her thoughts as she descended the stairs.

Why hadn't she told her father she was going down to the beach instead of sneaking out like an errant child? He would've forbidden it, certainly. But she wasn't a child. She was—

A twig snapped.

Priss stopped two steps from the bottom and stood perfectly still. She had a sudden, eerie feeling that she was being watched, but attributed it to the fact that she was uneasy about being out here alone after her father's edict. Which was ridiculous since she usually was alone now that walking any distance had become difficult for him. But perhaps he'd had a similar feeling, she thought, and that was why he'd been so adamant about her not walking on the beach tonight.

She looked around her, but saw no one

or nothing out of the ordinary. Why then did this strange feeling persist? She looked a second time to be sure she was still alone and then, despite her misgivings, put her foot down on the last step above the beach.

Another twig snapped.

Priss's stomach lurched with fear. Her mouth and throat went dry, her hands clammy, and her heart pounded in her throat. *Run!* was all she could think. But even as she turned to dash up the steps to safety, someone jumped out of the trees and onto the step behind her.

Before she could scream for help, a filthy, callused hand clamped over her mouth and a strong arm bound her about the waist. She tried to bite, but the hand was too suffocating and the hold pulling her backwards down to the beach was too tight. Her shawl fell off as she squirmed from side to side while clawing with her nails at both the hands and the arm that clutched her.

Priss sent out a silent cry for Henry as she was dragged across the sand.

Henry rode as if the hounds of hell were after him.

The assistant director of covert operations had caught him off guard late that afternoon. He'd just finished writing a report on his final assignment and was preparing to close his office for the day when George Ault arrived unannounced shortly before four o'clock. Accompanying Ault was the man who was going to replace Henry in the ranks.

Without waiting for an invitation, the gray-haired Ault had settled into one of the leather chairs facing Henry's desk and then waved his companion into the matching chair. Introductions were made, and then the assistant director asked Henry to bring the new man up to speed on the existing mission. With France spoiling for another war and England crawling with enemy spies, Henry had been hard at work putting together a list of French commanders and their English contacts to present to the minister of military intelligence.

Hoping that was all Ault had on his mind, Henry quickly gave his replacement the details and supplied him several names that might prove useful. And then, running late and still needing to dress for dinner with Priss and the Admiral, he stood to usher the two men out the door.

Unfortunately, that wasn't all.

Before Henry could see them on their way, the assistant director had nodded in the direction of the inlaid sideboard and announced that he could use a spot of brandy. The new man had echoed that desire. Eschewing a glass for himself, Henry had poured each of the men a splash and had barely restrained himself from pouring it down their throats in his eagerness for them to leave.

Ault had frowned at the stingy amount of brandy in his glass but refrained from remarking on it. Instead he had taken a small sip, smacked his lips in appreciation and then delivered a compliment to Henry from the director himself for a job well done in the Feaster matter. Before Henry could offer his thanks, Ault had gone into an excruciatingly long-winded explanation of the affair for the new man's benefit, and an increasingly impatient Henry had resumed his seat.

Lord Leslie Feaster had been England's ambassador to Paris. He'd also been deeply in debt, having inherited enormous tax liabilities along with his fine title. His position as ambassador had put him in the perfect spot to betray information about British troop and naval movements to the French in exchange for the money to ease his financial burden.

Another agent posing as Feaster's secretary, had noticed the ambassador carrying on a most peculiar correspondence describing his own travels about the Continent with a businessman who himself traveled extensively between Paris and London. The agent, his suspicions aroused, had sent a communiqué to the director, who in turn had put Henry on the case.

The message about Feaster's correspondence had provided the much-needed break in the long-standing situation. One of the things that had previously puzzled the service was that the traitor seemed to know exactly when and where those movements would be made. Early on, Henry had deduced that only a man high up in the service of England could be passing on the information, but it was a mystery as to who that man could be—until Feaster's "secretary" had handed over the copies he had written in his own hand of the ambassador's letters to the businessman.

Henry had spent several months working on deciphering the coded language in Feaster's letters, comparing his supposed travels with actual troop movements, and tracing the growing amounts of money that appeared in his bank accounts. Once he'd put it all together, Henry had shown the results to the director and suggested that a warrant be issued and an arrest made.

Feaster pled guilty to all charges but not before trying to justify his treason by claiming that the estates he had inherited from his wastrel father had come to him weighed down under such staggering debts that they were in danger of being sold at a creditor's auction. No one felt sorry for him, of course. To the contrary, the ambassador's two brothers and one sister had disowned him and his wife had packed up their three children and left him.

Once Ault finally finished his explanation, Henry accepted the director's compliments and, once again, came to his feet to see Ault and his companion out.

But Ault had had something more

on his mind. Something he believed Henry might be interested in hearing. Coming straight to the point for a welcome change, he'd said that Dos Sebastián's ship had been spotted earlier that week sailing near the entrance to the bay.

Ault was right. Henry *was* interested. He was also greatly alarmed. After the first flash of heat, everything in him turned to ice. There was only one reason the Spanish pirate would be anywhere near the bay, and that was to seek revenge for the boarding of his ship and the hanging of his crew all those years ago. How he'd found out where the Admiral lived was anyone's guess, but it didn't bode well for the old man.

Or for Priss, he thought now, his heart sinking with foreboding as he spurred his fleet black barb onward, toward the house that overlooked the bay.

Henry grimaced as he thought back. He'd decided only this morning that tonight he would seek the Admiral's permission to reveal his true self to Priss and to ask her to become his wife. He'd loved her when she was but a pretty little, high-spirited girl of five and he but a boy of twelve home from

Eton for a school break. They were both too young then for any romance, of course, so he'd always made certain he behaved more like an older brother than a potential lover. But he had kept a close eye on her, watching her grow in both spirit and beauty, through his studies at University and his work as a covert agent for England.

A crack shot and a skilled swordsman, Henry had given his all to King and County these past few years. He'd moved through a maze of intrigue and espionage, engaging the enemy with great success wherever he was dispatched. He was proud of what he'd accomplished for his beloved England. But after completing a particularly harrowing operation on the Iberian Peninsula, the director had given him a new assignment—an assignment with which he had bitterly disagreed.

The service needed a new face, a complete unknown, someone who was free to take up residence in London where he could pass for a dandy who wore his clothes perfectly, who acted pleasantly harmless, was dryly witty, and was invited to all the right places. It was a simple plan, the director told him, so simple that no one would ever suspect who he really was or what he was up to.

Though he'd first balked at the idea, Henry finally had to admit it was working quite well. He'd flitted from dinner party to weekend hunt to fancy ball, all the while playing the part of an innocuous fop. In the process he had gleaned valuable information from the wives and daughters of political or military figures and cultivated the friendship of men in high places. Occasionally he had burglarized desks and government offices in search of clues to identify foreign agents.

In return for acting the professional fool, he'd been given *carte blanche* to kill anyone who endangered the mission. The level of force he used was of his own choosing. Fortunately, he'd only had to use lethal force once, in self-defense. But never knowing for certain who plotted with him and who sharpened their knife to use against him, Henry was certain it was only a matter of time before he'd need to kill again.

The constant danger had been stimulating, but also limiting. An agent was better off without a family pulling him one way while his professional duties pulled him in another. Hence, his recent decision to leave the service, establish a full-time law practice, and reveal his feelings for Priss.

The irony was the Admiral asking him to make a list of possible suitors for her before he could tender his resignation, so to buy time until he could finish his final case and declare himself, he'd devised a scheme of his own. Three times he'd compiled lists filled with drunks and dandies, dice players and other sorts of dodgy candidates in hopes Priss would find something wrong with every one of them. To his relief, she'd done exactly that.

But now, driven by the fear that he'd dawdled too long, Henry tossed his horse's reins to the groom standing outside the stable, leapt down from his saddle and then dashed across the courtyard and into the house.

"Where is she?" he shouted to the household at large.

Will came running from the dining room, Alice from upstairs and Cook from the kitchen. All three came to a stop, staring with their mouths open at the man who stood so straight and tall in the spacious vestibule.

Henry looked nothing like the frippery

fellow they were used to seeing about the house. His powdered hair was now thick and black and shot through with bronze glints as it caught the fading sunlight shining through the open door. Wind-tousled and untied, it spilled over the unbuttoned collar of a full-sleeved white shirt that perfectly fit his broad shoulders and hugged his muscular torso. Dust streaked his buff-colored breeches and knee-high boots. Without the coating of white powder he normally wore, his face was tan and chiseled, with cheekbones that looked sharp enough to cut a finger and a jaw that appeared to be set in stone.

His gray eyes were hawk-fierce without the lorgnette he usually employed, and the normally pinched lips they'd grown accustomed to were drawn into a demanding line as his gaze flicked from one servant to the other.

"Where is she?" Henry repeated, resting his hand on the butt of the pistol he wore strapped to his waist. "Where is Miss Priss?"

"She wasn't on the balcony when I brought the Admiral's empty glass down," Will answered.

"She wasn't in her bedroom when

I laid out her sleeping gown and slippers," Alice added.

"She isn't in the kitchen," Cook added, wiping her steam-flushed face with her apron.

"She went to the beach," said a voice from on high.

Henry spun, his gaze traveling upward. The Admiral stood at the head of the staircase, immaculately outfitted in the navy blue and white uniform that still fit him and a pair of spit-and-polish boots.

"I saw her from my window," the older man said, "but I couldn't open it in time to call her back."

Henry wheeled sharply and sprinted out the door. He flew down the three sets of terrace steps to the beach. No sooner had he set foot on the sand than he collided with a staggering Odd the Vonck.

He grabbed the lapels of the pirate's filthy waistcoat and shook him hard. "Where is she? Where is the Admiral's daughter? What have you done with her?"

Vonck's head bobbed almost drunkenly back and forth, and his left arm hung uselessly at his side. "I-I ain't d-done nothin' with 'er. I swear. I-I never even s-seen 'er."

Henry finally noticed the badly swollen bruises at Vonck's temple and on his cheeks, the bright red blood dribbling from a deep cut over his good eye and more blood trickling out of his oft-smashed nose.

Realizing he was overwrought, he released the man and got a firm grip on his emotions. "What happened to you?"

"I was walking along the beach, like ye ordered, lookin' t' throw a scare into the gel, when someone clubbed me from behind." Grimacing, Vonck wiped the blood out of his eye with the hand of his good arm and then turned his head far enough for Henry to see the wound on the back of it. "I fell, and that's when I realized there was two of 'em. They beat me. Beat me bad. Broke me nose an' left arm in th' bargain."

Henry frowned, thinking hard. If Vonck hadn't seen Priss—

A slight breeze picked up a length of white silk near the water's edge and blew it in his direction.

He caught it in midair and recognized it as the shawl Priss liked to wear on her evening walks. A wave of guilt washed over him. He buried his nose in the silky fabric and inhaled her rose scent. He'd failed her, failed to arrive on time, failed to protect her, failed her in every earthly way. His heart thudded at the thought of what might have happened to her as a result.

"Dos Sebastián," Henry said grimly.

His hand trembling, Vonck wiped away a fresh dribble of blood from his broken nose. "Ye think that's who did this t' me?"

"Not him personally," Henry clarified. "More likely it was members of his crew acting on his orders." He thought back and then said, "Those pirates at The Mermaid—"

"The ones sittin' near us?"

It was the only thing that made sense to Henry. "They might have been part of Sebastián's crew."

"Mebbe so." Vonck shrugged. "I didn't recognize any of 'em but then it's been years since I seen that motley bunch."

"They must have overheard us talking and passed the information on to Dos Sebastián," Henry mused aloud.

"But we was talkin' quiet like," Vonck reminded him.

"Not quietly enough, it seems." Another more ominous thought hit Henry like a fist. "You said Sebastián was trading in slaves."

"That 'e is."

Fury edged in fear for his beloved welled inside Henry as he fingered the delicate material that had last touched Priss about her shoulders and arms, but he forced himself to keep his temper in check. "Where's the next slave auction?"

"The Barbary, I s'pose."

"Where on the Barbary?"

More blood trickled down Vonck's battered face as he shook his head.

"Would your quartermaster know?"

The pirate gave a pained grimace. "Me 'elmsman, more likely."

Henry tied the silk shawl about his waist so he could return it to Priss in person. He looked out beyond the bay, to the hated sea, before turning back to Vonck. "Where's your ship?"

"Across the bay, where ye told me t' leave it," he said through bruised lips.

Henry glanced up at the darkening sky and then grabbed Vonck's good arm with his free hand. Years ago he'd sworn to never step foot aboard another ship as long as he lived. But now Priss's life depended on him doing exactly that.

Ignoring the pirate's groans of pain, he started herding him along the beach, in the direction of his moored ship. "Come on, we're losing the light."

"I'm going with you."

Turning on his heel, Henry saw the Admiral standing on the bottom step. Stopping to catch his breath, the old man leaned his weight on the walking stick that his missing daughter had had carved for his last birthday. In his other hand, he held a brass-bound spyglass.

"Sir." Henry snapped his heels to attention, an old habit he thought he'd forgotten.

"What are we waiting for?" growled the former commander of his own fleet of British seabound forces as he squared his shoulders and limped goutily across the sand. "Let's go take Miss Priss back from that pirate."


*The Caribbean*


Victoria awoke, not to the brutal fumbling of a molester, but to the careful ministrations of an old man with grizzled hair and a concentrated expression on his face. Startled, she jerked upright, nearly upsetting the basin of pinkish water he'd placed beside her on the bed.

"Lay you back down, Lady, so I can see how badly you hurt," he said in the melodic accent of the Islands before bending his head over the steaming cloths in the basin.

She looked at him quizzically.

"Ship doctor," he said, answering her unspoken question.

Somewhat reassured, Victoria laid back down and let him finish cleaning her face. That done, he pushed up her torn sleeves and began removing the blood and the splinters from her forearms and hands.

"Lady all right," he finally pronounced, crossing the room to dump the basin of dirty water into a chamber pot.

Victoria felt a gentle, rhythmic rocking and was dimly aware of the creaking of timber. How much time had passed since the pirate had taken her prisoner? Hours? Days? She licked her lips and tried to ask, but the only sound she could make was a raspy croak.

"Water," the doctor said, pouring

her a glass from a pitcher that sat on a small table next to the door. "Nice and cool."

Pain burst through her head and her body as she clumsily levered herself into a sitting position and reached for the water. She choked at first, then swallowed and drained the glass. Her smoke-parched throat somewhat soothed by the water, she asked him in a hoarse voice, "How long have I been here?"

"Four, perhaps five hours."

It was then that she noticed she was sitting on a luxurious red taffeta quilt atop a bed built into the wall. "And where exactly am I?"

"In de captain's cabin."

Victoria glanced about her, thinking she had gone mad. This was no cabin! Or was it? She was in a beautiful room paneled in rich, reddish-brown wood. The fittings were burnished brass that shone from years of daily polishing. Against the wall across from the bed was a wide desk with a chart laid out atop it and other charts rolled and neatly filed in pigeonholes above it. Running along the back wall were the sparkling diamond-paned windows of the aftercastle.

Feeling a bit dizzy, she closed her eyes against the hot glare of the late day sun shining in from the windows. When she opened them again, a bank of cabinets and drawers with porcelain pulls built into one of the walls floated in and out of her field of vision and she realized she did not yet have the strength to focus.

She gave the glass back to the doctor, blinked at her bruised hand, and realized suddenly how dirty and disheveled she was. Sweat and soot and other people's blood stained her once-pristine dress. Her hair had fallen loose and hung in limp wisps around her face and her shoulders. Her stockings were ruined, and her shoes were gone.

"You are traveling alone?" the doctor asked her as he returned the empty glass to the table.

Victoria pushed her hair behind her ear. "My maid fell ill with a fever the day before we were scheduled to leave Martinique."

The doctor gave her a kind smile. "You were anxious to go home?"

"Yes, very."

He crossed to the desk, and Victoria sat up.

"Stay you there," he said as he opened the desk drawer.

"What are you doing?" she asked, a little angry at the way he kept ordering her around.

"Making sure Lady doesn't hurt herself," he answered, removing a gold letter opener and a small, sharp knife from the drawer. "De captain come soon."

His words struck terror in Victoria's heart. "The pirate captain? What would the pirate captain want with me?"

He only shrugged and tucked the opener and the knife in a pocket of his breeches.

"I'll be poor sport!" Victoria cried defiantly. "I'm dirty and plain!"

The doctor picked up the empty basin he'd used to tend her injuries and opened the door. Halfway out of the cabin, he turned back to look at her and said, "Lady not plain."

He punctuated that statement by shutting the door and shooting home the bolt.

# Chapter 8

*A* scurrying sound told Priss she was in the company of a mouse or—horrors!—a rat.

She shivered, but there was no way to avoid the creature. She was locked in a dark, tiny cubicle that must have normally served as a storeroom of some sort. There was no light leaking in from under the door or through the jamb so she couldn't tell whether it was night or day. Worse, there was practically no air.

Panic flared when something furry brushed against her foot. It took every ounce of her willpower to stifle a scream. She'd lost her shoes in the jolly boat, and her stockings had been shredded while fighting like an enraged lioness to be free from the pirates who'd grabbed her. She'd slapped one pirate in the face and stabbed another one in the arm with the knife she'd grabbed out of the sheath at his waist. All the while screaming Henry's name. For their own protection, the pirates had gagged her and tied her hands behind her back. Still, she'd managed to do considerable damage to several more of them with her feet and knees before they'd subdued her and rowed back to their ship.

The fight wasn't out of her even then. She'd twisted and rolled as they'd hauled her up the ladder that hung over the ship's side. She'd kicked the pirate below her in the nose, breaking it in a gush of blood. She'd worked the foul-tasting gag out of her mouth and almost bit off the index finger of the one above her. Her kidnappers were happy to unload her on the quartermaster, who'd ordered her untied and locked in the smothering darkness of the closet.

Once free of the confining ropes, she'd used her fingers to comb the wild disarray of her hair off her face, then hugged her knees tight to her chest and covered her bare feet with the skirt of her stained and wrinkled blue lawn dress to keep them from being bitten by rodents.

Priss knew she had no one but herself

to blame for her predicament. That was a bitter pill to swallow, and almost choked her going down. But it was the truth. If she hadn't slipped out of the house and down the steps to see what was happening on the beach, she wouldn't be crammed into this dark, stifling space with no room to stretch out and no idea of what might happen to her next.

She still didn't know why she had called out for Henry Oliver when she was taken. Beyond the starlit kiss that burned still in her memory, he'd never exhibited any untoward affection for her. Oh, he'd put her up on her first pony. Taught her the rudiments of chess and played innumerable patient games with her. Listened without interruption to her rambling stories. Fenced with her when she had no one else to practice with. He'd just always been there, dependable, efficient, and in the last few years, the Pinkest of the Pinks.

The more she thought about the unfailing love he exhibited for her father, the kindness Alice claimed he showed the servants, the occasional glimpse she caught of the man she'd known and, yes, loved all those years ago, the more she realized she had for some time had a growing awareness that there was more to him than met the eye—that beneath the outlandish clothes and eccentric mannerisms was a man of honor, a man whom a woman could depend upon in good times and in bad. She knew now that she would never look at Henry in quite the same way again.

*If* she ever saw him again.

What about her father? She worried that her disappearance would be the death of him. Already ill, he'd likely take to his bed and breathe his last.

And what was to become of her? Would she be killed? Sold into slavery? Abused by the pirate captain and then thrown to his underlings aboard ship? She'd never before experienced real fear. She'd been raised with love and affection, safe and secure in a lovely home where something as implausible as being kidnapped by pirates had never occurred to her.

Hunched over her knees in this dark, airless space, the possibilities of what the pirates might do to her sent waves of terror through her.

All because of her own insatiable curiosity.

Overwhelmed by guilt, Priss laid her forehead on her knees and closed her eyes. She conjured her father's face—proud, defiant, and filled with fervent fatherhood. Oh, why hadn't she just married one of the men on Henry's wretched lists and made her father happy? It wasn't so much to ask. He'd given her his time, his knowledge, his unconditional love. The least she could have given him was the pleasure of seeing her properly settled.

The tears she'd managed to hold at bay suddenly came in fiery torrents. She cried out of shame at her own selfish behavior, out of fear at what fate awaited her, and out of the heart-wrenching knowledge that she might never see her father again. Exhaustion finally claimed her, and she fell asleep.

She dreamed about Henry. Only he didn't look like the overdressed gadfly who served as her father's solicitor. He looked like her fictional pirate, with his hair whipping in the wind like black silk, his white shirt hugging his muscular torso, and a pistol riding upon his trim hip as he stood on the foredeck of a lateen-rigged and narrow-prowed ship that was racing to her rescue . . .

Henry hadn't intended to take command of Vonck's ship. He was no sailor. He'd spent years at the University in order to ensure he would never again have to return to the sea. But he couldn't walk across the water to rescue Priss. And with Vonck lying abed in sick bay, the quartermaster and several other crew members violently ill from gorging on raw oysters washed down with copious amounts of rum the night before, and the Admiral busy scanning the horizon with his spyglass for any sign of Dos Sebastián's ship, someone had to take command.

And take command was exactly what Henry had done.

Dos Sebastián had a full night's head start on them, so this morning Henry had bellowed and cursed and rousted the ailing crew with a razor's-edge callousness until the ship was safely out of the bay and on the open water. Only when full dark fell and the watchmen were posted did he stop to get something to eat and to check on the Admiral.

With Priss in peril and his nerves

wire-tight, Henry was too wound up to sleep. Vonck remained under the care of the ship's doctor, so Henry commandeered the captain's quarters for the Admiral. They were cramped but decently furnished with a desk and a chair, a sea chest along one wall, and a bed along another.

Once Priss's exhausted father was stretched out on the bed, Henry sat down in the chair, moved the stack of charts aside, and leaned back. Letting out an exhausted breath of his own, he'd put his heels on the desk, crossed one leg over the other, and locked his fingers behind his head.

"This is all my fault," the Admiral had said in the voice of one admonishing himself.

Henry had no words of comfort to offer. He was dealing with his own guilt. "If only I'd arrived on time for dinner, I—"

"Dos Sebastián was after me."

Henry didn't even try to deny it.

"Priss was simply in the wrong place at the wrong time."

And she was counting on him now, Henry could feel it. "We'll find her."

The old man swallowed audibly.

"He'll sell her in a slave market to spite me, and we'll never see her again."

"Over my dead body."

"You're going to kill him."

"Yes, sir," Henry vowed in a voice edged with revenge.

The Admiral had rolled over then and fallen into a deep sleep. Henry dozed off and on. In his waking moments he'd savored the thought of the Spaniard's impending death.

Finally the first gray light of dawn began to filter through the window and the sound of feet pummeling the main deck seeped into the cabin.

Henry stretched and yawned. His back and shoulders ached from the uncomfortable position in the chair. Glancing around, he saw that the Admiral was still asleep, so he left him in the arms of Morpheus and headed up to the foredeck.

The closest he'd come to the foredeck in his cabin boy days was when he'd sought a place to hide from the Spanish pirate's fists. Usually he could find a bolt hole under one of the sick bay beds or in the larder. Once he'd hidden in the ship's magazine. By the time he was discovered he was covered in gun powder. Dos Sebastián had ordered him tied up and repeatedly dunked in the sea until he'd nearly drowned. That had put an end to his attempts to escape the Spaniard's wrath. He'd simply taken the blows as they came until he was rescued.

Now, with every foot of the *Sea Devil's* canvas spread as it raced at a wind-wild pace to catch up with that same Spaniard's ship, Henry stood next to the thick-set helmsman who sported a bald head, a bushy red beard, and bowed legs.

"He can't be too far ahead of us," Henry remarked.

"Nay," the helmsman replied in heavily Scots-accented English.

Raising his hand to his eyes to shade them against the glare of the morning sun on the water, Henry scanned the horizon, searching for signs of Dos Sebastián's ship. Nothing greeted him except the empty sea.

He looked at the Scotsman who had charge of the wheel. "The problem is, we don't know for certain where he's going."

"Algiers'd be my guess," the Scotsman said, giving the wheel a turn to keep the ship a safe distance from a promontory that reached out from shore

"What makes you say Algiers?"

"Biggest slave market on the Barbary." While Henry mulled that over, the pirate added, "Them bashas and deys will pay a pretty price for an Englishwoman. There's somethin' about their smooth alabaster skin that sets their souls on fire."

Henry's heart pounded like a loose jib in the wind. Despite his inner turmoil, he kept his expression calm and his gaze steady. He couldn't let his emotions rule. He had to keep his head about him.

"How long do you think it will it take us to reach Algiers?" he finally asked.

"With a fair wind in our sheets, as we have now, and no storms to waylay us"—the pirate paused, figuring—"two, mebbe three weeks'd be my guess."

And if Dos Sebastián went somewhere besides Algiers? Henry stewed. They would have wasted two to three weeks. Priss might be lost to him, perhaps forever. Could he risk that? Could she survive—

There was no point in conjuring up worst case scenarios, he told himself. He would find her if he had to swim the seven seas.

Seeming oblivious to his companion's frame of mind, the helmsman returned to his previous topic of conversation. "They hide their female captives in harems, y'know."

An icy blast of fear blew through Henry at the thought. Priss was a fighter and wouldn't go willingly into a harem, but she wouldn't stand a chance against those potentates' guards. He'd heard plenty of horror stories about what they were capable of, but he couldn't bring himself to dwell on them right now.

"Leaves their families believin' they died." The sailor lifted his weighty shoulders in a fatalistic shrug. "Might be for the good, given what they suffer at the hands of them savages."

The very thought of it twisted Henry's stomach in knots. Priss was alive. He was sure of it. But for how long? He stared unseeing at the miles of open sea before them, molten in the rose and peach glow of the newborn day. Every mile took the woman he loved farther away from him. At the same time it brought him closer to her.

Somehow he would find her. He had to believe that. He forced himself to breathe slowly, to think. His head said there were maps and charts scattered all over the desk in Vonck's cabin, and the Admiral knew the seas like most people know the back of their hand. But his heart . . .

Decision made, he looked back at the helmsman's weather-tanned and hairy countenance and realized he was missing a vital piece of information. "What's your name?"

"Enda, sir. Enda MacKenzie."

"All right, Enda," Henry said, "let's go to Algiers."

*The Caribbean*

Hearing the departing doctor throw the bolt sent Victoria into a panic. Already half out of her mind with fear, she rolled off the bed and onto the wooden floor, and then began crawling on her hands and knees across the cabin. Reaching a wall, she clawed at the smooth wood paneling until she found purchase and could stand. The cabinets and drawers still seemed to float before her eyes. She reminded herself that she was not one of those silly fainting women. She must be calm—breathe deeply, slowly.

Yes, that was better. She could see things a bit more clearly now.

She took one step, then another, and ran into the desk. She stumbled and fell over it, losing her hard-won composure. They were going to violate her and torture her, make her tell who the rich passengers they'd kidnapped were so they could demand ransom. Rob, kill!

"No!" she sobbed, coming to her knees again and groping for the desk drawer. She yanked it open and rummaged through it with trembling hands, trying to find something besides the letter opener and the knife the doctor had confiscated earlier, hoping to discover something that she could use to kill herself before the pirate could abuse her.

Pieces of paper, money, a handful of jewels—aha, an ink bottle. She snatched it up, intending to break it and use its sharp edge to slit her wrists.

The ship pitched, throwing the ink bottle and Victoria onto the floor. She rolled until her head struck the leg of a chair on the other side of the desk. She laid still for a moment, gulping air. Looking up at the bank of windows along the back wall, she noticed that

110

the sky had a faintly dusky hue. The lantern the doctor had lit and left on the hook by the door cast eerie, elongated shadows upon the cabin's paneled walls.

"Ev'nin', Cap'n," said a voice outside the door.

Victoria sat up, looked down at her tattered, dirt-and blood-spattered dress and knew she resembled a scarecrow. She tried to scramble to her feet, but her knees were so wobbly she fell flat on her face as the cabin door banged open. Useless. She was useless. She swallowed a whimper of abject terror as heeled boots swaggered across the wooden floor, stopping near her head. She pushed back disheveled brown hair, propped herself on unsteady elbows and looked up into the amused gray eyes of her captor.

"Would you like a bath?" he asked her, with only the faintest trace of an accent marking his voice.

# Chapter 9

$\mathcal{T}$he storeroom door flew open. Daylight flooded in and nearly blinded Priss, causing her to shield her eyes with her hand.

"Git up," a deep voice growled at her.

It took her a minute, but she finally managed to push herself to her knees and then up, to stand on cramped legs and numb feet before a grimy little pirate with a bandana wrapped turban-wise about his head

He grinned toothlessly and produced a piece of rope. "Gimme yer 'ands."

"I won't fight you," Priss promised, her voice unsteady.

"Damme right ye won't." He tied her wrists together with intricate knots that left her feeling as if the circulation in her hands and arms had been cut off.

Taking the free end of the rope, he

pulled her, stumbling along behind him on bare feet in her ruined dress, out of the storeroom and onto the ship's deck.

Priss's knees threatened to give way when an ugly, motley crew of pirates surrounded her, leering at her. Some were missing teeth. Others had scars or tattoos or gaping sores. All wore lecherous grins that brought home her dire circumstances.

She shivered despite the hot sun beating down on her, and for a moment, she wondered if the best solution might be to jump overboard at the first opportunity. Then she reminded herself that she was an Admiral's daughter, that such an act of cowardice would forever dishonor him. She mastered her fear through sheer determination. With her hands tightly tied in front of her, she held herself erect, her head high, shoulders back, spine stiff, and kept her expression calm.

Suddenly the crowd parted and a luxuriantly mustachioed pirate with the pitiless black eyes of a raptor stood before her.

Priss felt the blood drain from her face at the sight of him. He wore no hat atop the dozens of gray-flecked black braids that framed his weather-leathered face. An old scar bisected one of his eyebrows, others crisscrossed his cheeks. Silver rings pierced his nostrils and the lobes of his ears. His thin mouth had a distinctly cruel set.

He was dressed with expensive simplicity—a white linen shirt, black breeches of rich fabric tucked into high, soft suede boots with scrolled sterling buckles. Three braces of pistols belted his red velvet waistcoat. Heavy, ornately engraved gold rings glittered on each of his index fingers. Though he appeared to be perfectly at ease, she noticed the way his right hand played restlessly along the carved wooden handle of the double-edged knife that hung at his side.

"Welcome aboard, *Senorita* Fitch," he said in a voice rich with echoes of Spain.

Priss moistened her lips and prayed her voice would remain steady as she asked, "Do I know you, sir?"

"You and I have not had the pleasure of meeting until today." A cynical smile broke upon his haughty lips. "But I am well acquainted with your father."

His words, coupled with his heavy accent, rushed through her ears like the low murmur of an autumn wind, bringing chilly forebodings. "You—you're—"

"Dos Sebastián." He executed a courtly bow, then straightened. "Some call me The Spaniard. Others"—he pointed a proud finger at the brightly-emblazoned flag flying on the mast—"the Hawk of the Sea. And still others . . ."

Lifting his shoulders in an exaggerated shrug, he held out his sword-scarred hands, palms up, and looked about him at his crew. They elbowed each other, sniggering, and nodded in unison.

". . .well, I will not repeat the names they use," the pirate captain went on, "but suffice it to say they are not very becoming."

Priss had studied fencing long enough to know how to exploit an opponent's weakness. Watching her captor preen and pose for his admiring band of thieves, she realized that he was quite vain. She hoped that meant he was also easily flattered.

Deciding it couldn't hurt to test the waters, she smiled and said, "And with good reason."

A collective gasp rose from his crew at her daring.

"What do you mean by that?" The Spaniard's question had a cutting edge that seemed to slice through her.

"Only that your reputation precedes you," she explained.

His eyes narrowed to slits. "My reputation?"

Priss met his visual challenge full on. "Your reputation as a thief rich with the treasures of scuttled ships and the price of slaves captured and sold to the highest bidder."

"Ah, yes," he said in the boastful tone she had hoped to hear. "And where did you learn that pretty lesson, *Senorita* Fitch? Is your father your preceptor?"

She stood tight-lipped and utterly composed, refusing to answer him.

"Of course he is." He shrugged again, indifferently this time, as if was no matter to him one way or the other. "Ah, well, I will deal with your father soon enough. Meanwhile—"

"Please, Captáin." Priss raised her painfully-bound hands as if in prayer.

"You dare to interrupt me?" His harsh tone and the scowl that rumpled his face gave her a moment's pause.

But, remembering her strategy, she

wrapped her request in a honeyed tone. "Would you be so kind as to loosen the rope?"

Someone in the crowd snickered. The Spaniard shot the ruffian a quelling look.

"I heard how fiercely you fought when you were seized," he replied to her. "You stole one of my men's knives and stabbed him in the arm."

"Yes, but—"

"You broke another's nose and kicked and hit and bit and hit several oth—"

"I'm not used to being abducted," she reminded him.

"And yet," he countered in a deadly calm voice, "they did not kick or bite or hit you in return, did they?"

"No," she reluctantly admitted.

"So now you are suffering for your resistance," he said in a disdainful tone.

Priss refused to beg, but promised, "I won't do it again, Captáin Sebastián."

He waved an imperative hand at the pirate who had brought her before him. "Take her to the aft cabin and feed her. But do not untie her until you are certain there are no weapons she can use against you or anyone else."

"Aye, Cap'n." Nodding, the pirate

grabbed the end of the rope to lead her away.

Priss dug in her heels and turned to Sebastián, "What do you propose to do with me?"

"You will see in due time," he said.

Fear stole through her at his vague reply, but she maintained a calm facade. "Will you be holding me for ransom?"

"Ransom?" His cold eyes narrowed and his teeth, small and sharp as rapiers, shone in a menacing smile beneath the mustache. "No, not ransom. For revenge."


*The Caribbean*


Shortly after the captain left, the doctor returned. He carried a scrolled tray into the cabin and elbowed the door shut behind him. A chart still covered the desktop, so he balanced the tray against his body with one hand and pulled out a sliding side shelf on which he set it.

Victoria sat on the side of the bunk, her bare feet not quite reaching the floor. Her stomach growled, but she watched without saying a word while he arranged a white china bowl covered with a clean rag, a porcelain-handled spoon, and a small glass filled with an amber-hued liquid that looked like rum into a place setting for her. But when she made to stand and approach the desk, he stopped her with a shake of his head

"Bath first." He crossed to the cabinet built into the corner. He opened a drawer, removed a bar of soap, a silver-encrusted glass bottle, a small tin of tooth powder and a basin of water, all of which he set atop the chart on the desk before going to the cabin door and opening it.

Three men stood outside with a large copper tub. Other men were lined up behind them with buckets of steaming water. The first three men pulled the tub into the room and the other men filed through, each pouring in his bucket of water and leaving without looking at her. The doctor placed two lengths of heavy absorbent toweling beside the tub, opened the glass bottle and emptied the sweet-smelling powder it contained into her bath water.

"You—in," he ordered, gesturing first at her and then at the tub. "And don't waste time," he said on his way out the door. "De crew coming back in one hour to remove de tub."

Victoria was beyond thinking, beyond considering what was happening. She stripped off what remained of her salt-water and blood-crusted dress along with her undergarments and her stockings, and stepped into the tub. Vapors of steamy, exotic perfume enveloped her. A sigh of pleasure escaped her as she slipped deeper into the soapy water and lay back against the wall of the tub. She remained like that, reveling in the clean English smell of hot, fresh water, until she remembered that she needed to make haste.

She washed her long brown hair and scrubbed every inch of her slender body before she stepped out and wrapped one length of toweling around her hair and the other around her body.

Her stomach rumbled, reminding her that she hadn't eaten so much as a mouthful since breakfast the day before. Wrapped in the towels, she crossed to the desk, took the rag off the bowl the doctor had set there, and saw that it contained what appeared to be a fish stew. She spooned up a bite. It wasn't the best stew she'd ever eaten. The fish was rubbery, the rice sticky, and there were bits of what she hoped were spices and not bugs floating in the stew. She ate it all.

When she finished eating, she sniffed the contents of the glass—the bold, slightly syrupy odor told her that it was indeed rum. The priest at her convent school substituted rum whenever he ran out of communion wine, so she was quite familiar with both the smell and the taste. Picking up the glass, she emptied it in one long, burning swallow.

After cleaning her teeth, Victoria finger-combed her wet and tangled hair back off her face and looked over her clothing. It was shocking to see how little there was left to save. Her shoes were at the bottom of the ocean and her stockings were a muddy, bloody mess. Her dress and petticoat were ruined, but the simple lace and muslin shift she had worn beneath them was salvageable. She put it on, rinsed her hands in the cooling bath water, and then rolled the toweling and the rest of her garments into a ball and left them beside the tub.

It seemed inconceivable that she was in this situation. Her life until now had consisted of a childhood in London, followed by years at the convent school in Martinique, all in preparation for meeting and marrying a suitable man when she returned home. She'd been terribly sad when her mother died, of course, but she'd never known strife or real fear. Kindness was all that had ever touched her. She'd been trained to be a wife and a mother someday and she knew nothing else. Nothing in her education had prepared her for a situation like this.

And yet here she was, captured by pirates and locked in the captain's cabin.

Victoria swallowed hard, determined not to surrender to the tears that welled up in her eyes. She was alone, with nowhere to go, no one to hide behind, and nothing but her own resourcefulness to depend on. For the first time in her life she had to look into her own heart and mind and soul to find the courage to survive whatever came her way.

At the rap on the door, she pulled the red quilt off the bunk and wrapped herself in it before she bade the crew to enter to remove the tub and the toweling. They left the door unlocked, which surprised her. Shortly after one of the men came back to turn the lantern down, leaving the cabin in soft, dancing shadows.

Exhausted in mind and body, Victoria looked longingly at the bed. It was too tempting to resist. Her head still hurt from where she'd hit it earlier, and her chest was filled with the heavy weight of fear. Still swathed in the quilt, she pulled back the soft linen sheet, slid under it and closed her eyes. In moments, she'd slipped into the bone-weary sleep of one who had come a long distance and who had farther still to travel.

# Chapter 10

—⁓—

Admiral Fitch stood at the foredeck rail, walking stick in hand and spyglass to his eye, gazing out across the swell of water that unfolded for miles around the ship. He hadn't realized how much he'd missed the sea and sailing. But to be standing on deck with the salt spray in his face, a stiff breeze ruffling his mutton chops, and the familiar pitch and sway of the ship beneath his widespread legs, was complete happiness.

Until he remembered why he was here.

"The sea is still in your blood, hey?" Henry asked as he joined him at the rail.

The Admiral continued his assessment of the horizon. "I always hoped I would come back to her again someday, but . . ."

"Not like this," Henry finished for him.

The Admiral merely nodded.

Henry wiped his face dry on his shirt sleeve. "And I always hoped I would never taste salt spray again,"

The Admiral lowered the spyglass and raised a brow. "Yet here you are."

"Aye," Henry said in a wry tone that drew a reluctant smile from the older man. "Did you sleep well?"

"Well enough, considering."

"Have you had anything to eat?"

The Admiral shook his head. "I'm not hungry."

"It won't do Priss any good for you to lose your strength," Henry reminded him.

"Salt pork and hardtack it is, then," the older man relented, and turned to go belowdecks. Then he stopped and looked back. "About those lists of eligible men you put together for me. Priss found something wrong with every one of those nodcocks."

"It seems so, yes," Henry agreed.

"Was that your intention?" The Admiral gave him a look that said he already knew the answer to his question.

Henry didn't bother denying it. "She

told me when she came back from London that she had decided she would only marry a man she loved."

The Admiral raised a brow. "And she told me that she would wait forever, if necessary, for that man."

Henry flinched but didn't look away.

"It seems to me that Priss has waited long enough for you, Henry," the Admiral said before he turned away in search of breakfast.

Henry opened his mouth, then closed it and watched the older man limp away. How long had he known? More important, did Priss have any idea what he'd been up to? But he didn't have time to pursue the answers right now. He had a ship to command and a mission to complete.

Shading his eyes with his hands, he looked up at the crow's nest. The lookout gave him an "all's well" salute. The quartermaster, having recovered enough from his overindulgences of two nights ago had everyone stepping lively. Sailors checked riggings, mended shrouds, or polished cannons. Some of them whistled as they worked. Others cursed. Still others sang. The raucous laughter of circling gulls and the flapping of sails in the wind added to the music of the sea.

It was a perfect day for sailing

That thought took him back in time, to another perfect day for sailing. And to the starlit evening that had followed . . .

It was his last day home before he left for London and his first assignment as a covert agent. Only the Admiral knew when and why he was leaving. Henry hadn't had the heart to tell Priss the cover story he'd cooked up to account for his absence. Better he just leave and let her move on with her life, perhaps find a good man to marry, even if it cost him the greatest price he'd ever paid.

With that in mind, he'd allowed her to set the agenda for the day. They spent part of the morning fencing and part of it riding horseback before sharing a light lunch with her father. And then, even knowing his aversion to the sea, she'd pleaded and cajoled and had finally talked him into going sailing with her. After a sunny afternoon upon the open water, they turned toward the bay.

A sudden tempest howled out of nowhere. They were swept back out to sea and whirled about like spindrift.

Lightning slashed the skies, thunder rattled the boat and their nerves, and rain pounded down like the hammers of the devil's anvil, soaking them to the skin. They fought the wind and the waves trying to stay afloat until, as quickly as it had come, the storm was gone. By then night had fallen, the clouds had parted, and they were able to sail into the bay with the silver moonlight to guide their way.

"We made it!" Priss exulted when they finally reached the beach.

"We did, indeed." Standing, Henry kicked off his boots, peeled off his stockings and rolled his trousers up to his knees. He leaped out of the boat, into the remaining hem of water, and dragged them safely onto the sand. Then he turned and held out his hand to help Priss alight.

She, too, had removed her sodden stockings and slippers and pulled the pins from her long, wet hair. Leaving it all on the floor of the boat, she took his hand, picked up the dripping, dirty skirt of her dress and started to climb out. Her foot hit the edge of the seat and she stumbled.

He caught her about her slender waist

to steady her and then lifted her out. She responded by placing her hands on his shoulders, tilting her head at a tempting angle and looking at him expectantly as he lowered her to the sand. It was an intimate embrace, made even more so by the stars blooming above them in the night sky.

Henry told himself to release her, warned himself not to kiss her. Priss was only sixteen. She still had her come-out to experience, still had balls and parties to attend, still had society's finest to greet and men to meet. He'd already graduated from university and would leave on the morrow to begin his work as one of the Crown's spies.

Instead, he had thrown caution to the wind and pulled her closer, reveling in the feel of her lithe and lovely body pressed against his. Her earnest gaze locked with his. He felt himself lost in those beautiful blue eyes of hers, in the cream of her cheeks, the soft pink of her lips.

"Kiss me, Henry," she said in a voice that was neither coy nor cloying but that of a girl who had just become a woman before his very eyes.

"Priss . . ." He knew he'd never forget how enticing she looked in the moonlight, and it tore at his heart that he was soon to leave her.

"Kiss me," she repeated, her arms curving around his neck and her fingers threading through the damp hair at his nape.

No, he shouldn't be doing this, Henry chastised himself, even as his mouth came down on hers to claim her lips in a first kiss that would, he knew, likely be their last . . .

Eight bells rang, signaling the end of the four-hour watch and snatching Henry back to the present. He'd been right to leave her all those years ago. It had been too much to ask her to wait for him for uncertain months, maybe even years while he trotted off on some dangerous mission. The world he lived in had no place for someone like Priss.

But as of yesterday he didn't live in that world anymore.

And yesterday his nerves had quivered all day, even during his meeting with the assistant director and his replacement. It had taken every shred of self-discipline he possessed not to walk out on them and ride like the devil to the house on the hill. When he finally arrived and the Admiral told him that Priss had slipped out, alone and unprotected, he knew she was in danger. Grave danger, if his instincts were right. And his instincts had never failed him.

His mouth set in a hard line, Henry stared out at the vast expanse of sea that separated him from the woman he loved with all his heart.

"You don't have much longer to wait, Priss," he vowed into the bright morning sunlight. "Mark my words."

# Chapter 11

⁓

𝒫riss waited in the aft cabin, her stomach churning more from nerves than from hunger, for what seemed like hours. Finally, a pirate with rotting teeth brought her a tray of breakfast. Or was it lunch? She didn't know. She'd lost track of time and the small window on the far wall was so dirty she couldn't see out of it.

She approached the meal set upon the small table. The tray that held it was silver and badly in need of polishing. The plate was delicate white bone china, the eating utensils had mother-of-pearl handles, and the glass was a feather-light crystal goblet with a gold rim. But the food was inedible: leathery-looking strips that she supposed were some kind of meat, a glutinous lump of white stuff that must've been rice, and a dried-up wedge of lemon completed the meal.

Fortunately, the wine was cold and clear and delicious.

A different pirate came back to retrieve the tray. He looked surprised that the food was untouched but said nothing. Before she could ask him if she could have a wet cloth to wipe her face and hands and a comb to tame her tangled hair, he left, slamming both the door and the outside bolt into place behind him.

Priss looked about the sparsely furnished cabin with an eye for escape. In addition to the table, which was nailed to the floor and a chair that wasn't, there was a narrow bed covered with a colorful patch-worked quilt built into the wall. An unlit lantern hung next to the door and a chamber pot sat in the corner.

Maybe she could hide behind the door and use the pot to knock out the next man who came into the cabin, she thought. But then what? Where would she go? What would she do?

Or maybe she could sneak up onto the deck after dark and lower herself over the side. She was a good swimmer, so it might be possible to get away from the ship. But first she would have to get past all those ugly pirates who swarmed all over the place. Even if she did manage to get that far, there might be sharks in the water. Or what if no other ships came along to pick her up and take her home? How long would she last in the hot sun and the salty water?

No, she decided. She'd wait. Eventually, Dos Sebastián would remember she was here and would let her know how he planned to exact his revenge.

There was no escape—at least not yet. Feeling dirty and hungry and drowsy from the wine, Priss decided to take a nap. She didn't turn back the quilt for fear of what she'd find beneath it but simply lay down atop it and closed her eyes. Hours later, she awoke to a knock on the door.

"Come in," she called as she sat up on the edge of the bed.

"Evenin', Miss," said a thin red-haired boy in threadbare clothes who stepped into the cabin, turned his back to her, and lit the lantern that hung on a hook by the door.

"What time is it?" she asked around a yawn.

The boy tipped his head as the piercing sound of a whistle piped the change of duty. "Eight o'clock."

When he turned around, she noticed his bruised eye. She shook off the last vestiges of sleep and frowned at him. "What happened to your eye?"

He waved off her concern with a casual, "Cor, Miss, t'aint nothin'."

"Who hit you?"

"The Cap'n, Miss." He gave her an apologetic smile, and she saw that one of his front teeth was chipped.

"The Captain?" she repeated, aghast.

"Cuffed me for not bringin' 'is wine fast enough."

Priss felt a surge of anger on the boy's behalf, but kept her tone of voice neutral. "What's your name?"

"Tommy."

"Tommy what?"

His face scrunched up in thought. "I don't rightly recall, Miss."

Priss resisted the urge to reach out and pat his shoulder in a gesture of comfort. "How old are you, Tommy?"

"I ain't sure, Miss." He scratched his shaggy head. "Eleven. Mebbe twelve."

She had guessed as much as he had all the gangly qualities that went with that age. "Why did you join this crew?"

"I didn't—not willingly, anyway." He shrugged his bony shoulders. "I was kidnapped off the street on me way t' school, as were many other boys. I jumped ship  first chance I got but was caught again. That's when I ended up on the slave block in Algiers—"

"Algiers!" she gasped, having read of the atrocities that happened there.

He nodded. "Cook says we're going back."

"To—?"

"Algiers."

Priss tried to swallow, but fear had dried up the moisture in her mouth and throat. This was to be Dos Sebastián's revenge against her father, she realized. He had ordered his crew to kidnap her, and now he was going to sell her to the highest bidder.

*I have got to get off this ship*! If she wasn't rescued, she *had* to find a way to escape. Surely she could find a way to escape if she wasn't rescued. Reading and hearing the horror stories of people being sold in slave markets was one thing, but the thought of possibly being auctioned off in one herself . . .

"Anyway," Tommy continued, clearly unaware of her inner turmoil, "I was sold to the Cap'n, and he signed me on this ship as a cabin boy."

Priss couldn't help but think of Henry, who had suffered a similar fate under the very same pirate. "Do you have a family to go home to, should you be able to escape?"

The spasm of sadness that rumpled his face made her regret the question. "I do, Miss, but they've probably forgotten all about me."

Before she could give in to the emotion that constricted her throat, her growling stomach reminded her she hadn't eaten today. "Tommy, could you by chance find me some food?"

"O' course!"

"A wet cloth, too," she added. "Oh, and a comb."

While Tommy went in search of food and her other requests, Priss pressed her stained and wrinkled dress with her palms and finger-combed her hair. She felt like a bundle of used scrub rags. Scullery rejects. What she wouldn't give for a change of clothes, some stockings, and a pair of shoes.

"'Ere ya go, Miss." Tommy came racing back into the cabin with a dripping wet cloth in one hand and a comb that was missing about half its teeth in the other.

"Thank you, Tommy."

Nodding, he turned on his heel and dashed out again.

Priss scrubbed her face and hands before combing some of the snarls out of her hair. By the time she finished, Tommy had returned with a white china bowl of thickened pea soup; though strained, it contained foreign bits of unthinkable matter that made her shudder. He set the bowl on the table, then pulled a gold spoon and a couple of weevily biscuits from one pants pocket and a chunk of cheese that looked a tad moldy from the other pocket.

"Be right back." He ran out of the cabin again, then came back with a glass of wine and a small orange that looked quite edible.

Priss hadn't had anything to eat in over twenty-four hours, and she was starving. She gobbled up the soup and biscuits and cheese, washing them down with that delicious wine. Feeling much better, she peeled the orange and shared it with Tommy, who was now sitting cross-legged on the floor.

"Thank you so much, Tommy," she

said, wiping her mouth and hands on the wet cloth.

He swiped the sleeve of his faded shirt across his mouth. "Cap'n'ld kill me if 'e knew I gave you that orange. He keeps 'em 'idden in 'is cabin with some o' 'is other treasures."

She leaned forward and whispered, "It will be our secret then."

He gave her a quick, conspiratorial smile. "Yes, Miss."

"Please," she said, "call me Priss."

The watchman on deck shouted out that it was half past nine.

Tommy began gathering up her dirty dishes, but left the wet cloth on the table. "I'd best be goin'."

"Thank you for everything." She hesitated and then added, "I hope you'll come back tomorrow."

"I will, Miss Priss."

She waited until Tommy closed and bolted the door before moving the chair to the small window and climbing up on it. Using the wet cloth he'd left her, she wiped the filthy pane until she could see out. Not that there was much to see. There were clouds covering the moon and the stars, while only a faint blot of yellow from the stern's riding lantern dotted the dark water.

139

Priss squinted, hoping and praying that she might see the shape or shadow of a ship coming to her rescue. But when the clouds thinned, a tiny slice of melon moon cast its subtle light upon the dark and empty sea. She swallowed the fist-sized lump in her throat, determined not to give in to the disappointment that threatened to overwhelm her. Her life depended on keeping her wits about her, so she couldn't let her emotions have the upper hand.

Her emotions had betrayed her before . . .

She still remembered the morning she had awakened to learn that Henry was gone. Foolishly, she had imagined that their kiss had changed everything. That he would be sitting with her father at the table in the breakfast parlor, that they would gaze lovingly into each other's eyes, that he would have already declared himself and received her father's permission to marry her. She had dressed quickly and sailed downstairs, eager to see her beloved. Her heart pounding with expectation, she'd entered the breakfast room.

Only to find her father sitting alone at the table.

"Where's Henry?" she'd asked him, masking her disappointment with a small smile.

"He's gone," her father said gently.

"Gone?" she gasped. "Gone where?"

"To London. He's accepted a position there."

Priss had felt a blackness closing in on her. It had smothered her. She'd found it difficult to breathe. "That's impossible." Her words were barely audible. "He didn't say goodbye to me."

Concern etching his face, her father had stood and taken a step toward her. "He thought it best if he left—"

She'd retreated a half step, then turned on her heel and run out of the house to the stables. The truth had hit her hard when she saw that the stall where Henry kept his horse when he was visiting was empty. She'd wanted to cry, to scream, to throw herself on the dirt floor and pound her fists against it. Instead, she'd run back into the house, up the stairs, and locked herself in her room, crying until she had no more tears to shed. It was much later in the day before she emerged from her room, red-eyed but with her emotions finally under check.

Eventually, Priss had come to realize how naive she'd been. Henry wasn't the one who had instigated their kiss. She was. Henry hadn't said he loved her. She had simply assumed he did. Henry hadn't made any promises not to leave. In fact, he had left first chance he got.

And the pain of his long-ago rejection stung her yet.

Still, she had to believe that the man she'd loved since she was barely out of the schoolroom, the man who had kissed her one night and gone missing the next morning without telling her why or goodbye, the man for whom she'd tossed away so many years and so many potential suitors in the hope that he would someday come to his senses and come back to her . . . that man would never leave her at the mercy of the pirate he hated with a passion.

"Hurry, Henry," Priss whispered to the night-blackened water. "I'm still waiting for you."

*The Caribbean*

A discreet tap at the door woke Victoria. Still wrapped in the quilt, she sat up, dragged the sheet up to her chin in an attempt at modesty, and called out in a groggy voice, "Come in."

The doctor stepped into the room. Making an obvious point of speaking to the paneled wall just above her left shoulder, he said, "You would like breakfast?"

"Breakfast?" Victoria looked at the bank of windows and was amazed to see the pinkish light of dawn breaking through their leaded glass panes. She couldn't believe it. She'd slept all night! Or maybe longer . . .

She shook her head to clear it and then swallowed, trying to relieve her dry throat. "How long have I been asleep?"

"Since your bath."

"Yesterday?"

He shook his head. "Day before."

It took Victoria a moment to comprehend the fact that she'd slept almost forty-eight hours.

"Breakfast," the doctor reminded her.

Her stomach rumbled. "Yes, please."

"Coffee or tea?" he asked on his way to the door.

"Tea," she said, though in truth she was thirsty enough to drink either one.

"Sugar, but no milk," he warned her.

"No sugar, please." She'd never been fond of sweet tea.

"I find you something to wear, too," he said, and closed the door.

Victoria remained in the bed, clutching at the sheet, until he returned with some articles of clothing draped over his shoulder and an elaborately worked cloissoné tray in his hands. The aroma of freshly-baked bread started her stomach growling in earnest, and the large mug promised the beloved taste of tea. Once again, the doctor pulled out the desk's sliding shelf, placed the tray on it, and turned the captain's chair for her to sit in. Then he crossed to the bed and laid the clothes at the foot of it.

"De clothes clean enough. You put on when I leave." So saying, he made for the door.

"Doctor?"

He turned back, his grizzled eyebrows raised attentively.

"Are the men who survived and the women—the other women, I mean, and the children . . ." She swallowed hard before continuing, "What will happen to them? Are they all right?"

"Dey safe belowdecks," he assured her.

"Will they be held for ransom?"

Looking surprised at the idea, he shook his head. "No ransom."

She asked again, "Then what will happen to them?"

"Dey be put off on a deserted beach—"

"Marooned?" She recoiled at the thought..

"It be on de British shipping route, so dey just have to wait for a ship to pick dem up and take dem home."

"How long will that take?"

"A month. Two at most."

*Months?* Victoria's head spun at the very idea. "How will they survive in the meantime?"

He enumerated the ways. "Catch and cook fish, eat berries and fruits and nuts, drink from de fresh pool of water."

"Are there natives?"

"None I know of."

She couldn't repress a shudder. "It all sounds so . . . so—"

"Pagan?" he asked with a half-smile.

"Primitive," she said instead.

"At least dey safe," he pointed out.

"And me?" she asked, anxiety

suddenly blossoming inside her. "Will I also be allowed to disembark?"

He shrugged and opened the door. "I find you shoes, too."

Victoria tamped down her trepidation at the doctor's non-answer and left the comfort of the bed to get dressed. She put on a pair of black knee breeches and a red-and-white striped shirt. The breeches were too big even with her shift bunched up beneath them, so she pulled them up as high as she could and tied the tails of the shirt around her waist to keep them from falling down around her ankles. Wishing she had a ribbon to tie back her hair as well, she finger-combed it off her face and tucked the sides behind her ears.

Her stomach reminded her yet again that there was food to be had, and she headed for the desk to eat her breakfast. Having never worn anything but skirts, even in the heat and humidity of Martinique, she found she rather enjoyed the ease of movement the breeches provided.

Victoria removed the cloth that covered the tray, and was delighted to see that in addition to a small loaf of warm, crusty bread, there was a wedge of yellow cheese as well as a delicate silver knife with which to cut it. No sooner had she covered her lap with the cloth and picked up the knife to cut herself a slice of bread and a piece of cheese than the cabin door came crashing open and the pirate captain strode in.

The bath brigade followed behind him. Two men carried in the empty copper tub she had used two days ago and set it on the floor. Then the men who had lined up in the passageway marched in one by one and began filling it again.

Ignoring her as well as the rest of them, the pirate captain whistled as if he hadn't a care in the world as he crossed the cabin to the built-in cabinet. He rummaged through one drawer and then another. Finally he turned up a clean shirt and breeches and tossed them atop the bed that Victoria had recently vacated.

She watched in astonishment when he began undressing in front of her. She had never seen anyone naked except herself, and he peeled off his filthy, torn shirt as if there was nothing at all strange about doing so. Even as she sat staring at him in disbelief, she found herself almost admiring his strong sun-browned physique. Suddenly in the luxurious but compact ship's cabin he seemed larger, his shoulders broader.

Her face burning with embarrassment, Victoria forced herself to look away, to focus on the chart that covered the desktop. She wasn't looking for anything in particular, and she didn't understand what all the dots and Xs and ink blotches on the page in front of her represented. She simply wanted to focus on something else while her captor removed his breeches and stepped into the tub, noisily sloshing water over the side and onto the floor.

A grumbling stomach reminded her that breakfast was waiting. She cut a slice of the warm bread and a piece of the hard cheese and took a bite of each. When she looked back at the chart, something she hadn't noticed before caught her eye.

"You're not wearing shoes," the pirate captain commented.

Victoria startled. But keeping her gaze riveted on the chart, she swallowed a sip of the strong black tea before answering him. "I lost them when you attacked our ship."

He said something else but it didn't register because the bold black circle around the words "*James Bond*" on the chart in front of her held her fast . . .

# Chapter 12

⌇⌇

*T*ommy brought breakfast and a message from Dos Sebastián.

"Cap'n wants t' see you." He put a covered tray on the table and then pulled an orange out of one pocket and a clean wet cloth out of the other.

Apprehension shivered through her, but Priss maintained the calm facade she'd exhibited for the past two days as she wiped her face and hands with the cloth. "Did he say why?"

The boy shook his head, and she noticed a new bruise on his jaw. It infuriated her to think of the Spaniard hitting him, but she had no idea what she could do about it. He was a captive, just like her, and they neither one had the power or the resources to overcome the pirate crew.

She peeled the orange and offered a

segment to Tommy. "I'll eat and then we'll go."

With the exception of the orange, the food was inedible. Priss took one bite of salt pork and barely managed to gag it down. The sea biscuit was so hard she feared she'd break a tooth, so she only nibbled around its edges.

She pushed the tray away and stood. "I'm ready."

Tommy grabbed what remained of her half-eaten biscuit and gnawed off a big bite as he led her down some steps and through a dimly lit passageway to the furthest door. He knocked once and the Spaniard bade entrance. The boy opened the door for her and then withdrew, closing it behind her as she stepped inside.

Priss stood with the door at her back, blinking in the sunlight that streamed through the diamond-paned windows along the back wall. The cabin was as colorful as its occupant, with vermillion-painted paneling scalloped with gilded edges and grinning golden gargoyles. A pair of perfectly matched Toledo cutlasses, blades polished to a wicked gleam, were mounted crosswise above a massive, chart-strewn desk that stood against the side wall. A bronze astrolabe in a wooden stand sat on the far corner of the desk, and two books stacked one atop the other on the near corner.

A vision in violent purple, brilliant yellow, and stark black, Dos Sebastián rose from the leather captain's chair. His purple vest was shot through with silver threads and sported scrolled silver buttons. It was worn under an unbuttoned black waistcoat stiff with purple-stitched lining. The small explosion of yellow silk at his throat served as a cravat, and the amethysts in his ears were as big as walnuts. Two black belts, one that held a scabbard and sword and the other a pistol completed his attire.

"Come in, *Senorita* Fitch," he said, with a polite bow from the waist.

Not quite trusting this courteous version of her captor, Priss took only one step closer.

"You slept well?" he inquired.

"No," she answered shortly.

The Spaniard tipped his head back and forth but said nothing.

"Tommy said you wanted to see me," she reminded him.

Dos Sebastián appeared to take no notice of her response as he picked up the top book on the desk, opened it and turned the pages slowly and with great gravity. Then he closed it, reached for the other book and, holding one in each hand, he showed them to her.

"It is true that you wrote these books?" he asked.

Shock rendered Priss speechless as she stared at the books, bound in that familiar blue with the title and her name printed in gold on the spine. She took a deep breath, trying to regain her usual control. "Where did you get those?"

"In your village store."

"You bought my books?" Priss felt a small swell of authorial  pride at the thought.

The Spaniard's mustache fluttered in sardonic amusement. And suddenly, the truth struck at her like a blow as she remembered Cook telling her that a band of thieves had robbed the village store late one night shortly before she was kidnapped. She stared at him, stung to anger.

"You . . . you *pirated* my books," she said in a cold voice.

"My humble apologies, *Senorita* Fitch." He sounded anything but sorry as he set the books aside and turned back to her. With another one of those faux-chivalrous bows, he reminded her, "In case you have forgotten, it *is* what I do for a living."

"Committing acts of piracy against my countrymen."

"Your countrymen, others' countrymen . . .." He shrugged a dismissive shoulder. "I do not discriminate. I steal from everyone."

"One day," she warned him, "they will catch you again."

"And I will escape again." He wandered to the windows in the stern and looked out, his back to her. Then he turned to face her and gestured to a wooden chair cushioned in a hideous bile-green material that sat next to the desk. "Please."

Still wondering why he had summoned her, Priss sank into the chair.

He sat, too. Leaning back in his chair, he stretched out his legs and tented his fingers, studying her across the small space that separated them. "I must confess that I did not realize when I stole the books that the author was the daughter of my sworn enemy."

Priss remained silent, but his statement hit her with a stab of distress.

"I rarely steal books," he went on.

"Especially books written in English, a language I do not read as well as I speak."

"Why are you telling me this?" She couldn't help but ask.

The Spaniard sat forward, opened the bottom drawer of his desk, and pulled out a bottle and two silver tankards. He poured golden rum into one and offered it to her. When she refused with a silent shake of her head, he returned the bottle and the other tankard to the drawer, closed it, and then took a deep draught before setting the tankard down.

"I have never met an author before. But when I realized I had captured one"—his lips curved in a slow smile under his thick mustache—"I decided it was the perfect opportunity."

"The perfect opportunity for what?"

"For you to write a book about me," he said matter-of-factly.

She blinked in disbelief. "You want *me* to write book about *you*?"

The brilliance in his dark eyes answered her question.

"But outside of the fact that you escaped when my father arrested you all those years ago, I don't know anything about you," she protested.

He waved off her concern. "I will tell you what you need to know."

"It can take a long time to write a book—months, sometimes a year," she added, hoping to glean some idea of how much time she had to plot an escape, be rescued, or worse, sold into slavery in Algiers.

"Just a story about me, then," he said irritably. "A whole book would take too long."

Priss tried a different approach. "I have nothing to write on."

He opened the middle drawer of his desk and drew out some paper.

"And nothing to write with."

Out of a side drawer he took a pen and a small pot of ink and set them atop the paper.

Priss fell silent, having run out of delaying tactics. She gazed thoughtfully into the middle distance. His assumption that she would be willing to write his story was further proof of his arrogance.

But now that the shock had worn off, she realized he'd presented her with an opportunity. For one, to learn about the life of an actual pirate. Those details would add authenticity to the novel in progress sitting on her desk at home.

And for another, it gave her bargaining power to obtain a few of the things she wanted. Things like a bath, some decent food, and clean clothes. Perhaps a chance to free Tommy from Sebastián's cruel clutches and have him tend to her needs exclusively.

She had to keep her wits about her and be careful not to overdo it. If he thought she was trying to play him for a fool, he might lock her in the supply closet again. Or condemn her to something worse, like throwing her to his men or forcing her to walk the plank.

A quick plan formed.

"I'm so sorry, Captáin," she said with just the right amount of regret in her voice.

"Sorry?" he asked without any hint of the distrust she'd feared. "Sorry for what?"

She held out her hands, palms up, in appeal. "I'm so dirty and smelly and hungry, I couldn't concentrate on writing my own name much less writing a story about someone as important as you . . ."

That did the trick. A little over two

hours later, Priss found herself freshly bathed, shampooed, and well-fed on cold meat, fresh bread, and cheese, all washed down with another glass of that delicious wine.

She'd already donned the shirt that was more of a mottled gray than white and the rough black breeches that Tommy had found in the slop chest. He'd sworn they were clean, and a few wary sniffs had told her they were more musty than dirty. The heavy buckled shoes he'd brought cut at her heels, but they'd do.

As ready as circumstances permitted, Priss sat down at the table in her cabin, dipped her pen in the ink pot and began to write.

*The Caribbean*

Victoria finally figured out why there was a circle around the name of the ship on the chart in front of her. "You attacked the *James Bond* on purpose!"

"Of course I did," her captor said, making it sound as if it were a foregone conclusion.

"But why?"

"For the treasure."

158

She ventured a look back at the pirate captain, who was smiling at her as if amused by her astonishment. He was dressed now in a tan muslin shirt, tawny brown breeches, and three-quarter boots. His dark hair was still damp and was tied back off his face with a leather cord. A gold earring adorned his left ear and the handle of a silver dagger glimmered in the leather sheath at his waist.

"What treasure?" she demanded, irritated with herself for noticing the details of his appearance. "The *James Bond* was a merchant vessel," she reminded him in a clipped voice. "It was carrying passengers and sugar and rum and—"

"And gold and silver."

Victoria looked askance at that. "Where would it get gold and silver? And why?"

He raised a challenging brow. "You doubt me?"

She gave her head a nervous shake, then a nod, and then another shake. "No, but—"

"Would you like to see proof?"

"Yes," she said without the least bit of hesitation. "Yes, I would."

"You'll need shoes." So saying, he

crossed to the door and opened it just as the doctor approached with a pair of clogs in hand.

"Where are we going?" she asked as she stepped into the clogs.

"To the hold," he said, closing the door behind them.

The too-big clogs threatened to fall off her feet if she walked too fast, so Victoria shuffled along behind him down the dimly lit passageway. Following her were two burly crewmen who carried ropes as well as lanterns that cast lurid shadows on the walls. One of the crewmen grumbled something about women being bad luck on board a ship and the other one grunted his assent, but she ignored the comment and kept up with the captain as best she could.

Downward the four of them went, closer and closer to their destination. Finally they came to a trapdoor with a heavy iron ring.

The captain wrested the trapdoor open, gazed down into the woolen darkness, and then ordered one of the crewmen to hand him the end of a rope.

"Let me down slow," he ordered before beginning his descent.

A speechless Victoria watched him disappear into the Stygian silence.

"Now lower me a lantern," he called up.

Orange oil light soon beamed up from the darkness below, followed shortly by the jingle of what sounded like keys as well as the creak and the squeak of wood.

"And now the woman," he said when the noise subsided.

"Hold tight," the crewman instructed her as he handed her the rope.

"Don't look down," the other one said.

Victoria's stomach turned over at their orders. She'd never done anything as daring as this in her entire life, and all she could think was that she might lose her grip and fall. She swallowed hard, wiped her clammy palms on the legs of her breeches, and grasped the rope, holding onto it so tightly that her nerves vibrated with the strain. She was afraid to look down, afraid it would make her dizzy and cause her to plummet to her death, so she squeezed her eyes shut as she began her descent. She lost her clogs, one hitting the floor below from the sound of it, and the other one—

"Ouch!"

The other one hitting the pirate captain.

"You can let go of the rope now," he said as he caught her about the waist and lowered her gently to the floor.

But his hands continued to circle her waist even after she released the rope. His dark gray eyes held hers as well, and she was filled suddenly with an excitement hitherto unknown to her. She could feel a combination of strength and gentleness in his hands, could almost envision him pulling her even closer and taking her into his arms—

Shocked by that thought, she lurched back and he let her go.

He glanced down at her bare feet then and flashed a wicked devil's grin. "You've lost your shoes."

"Again," she said, and surprised herself by laughing as she stepped into the ill-fitting clogs that he'd set side by side on the floor for her.

He chuckled, a deep and throaty rumble, as he gestured for her to turn around.

Victoria had no words for the things she saw when she did so. He'd already opened the long row of shipping chests that she recognized as having been carried off the merchantman by his crew. The gaudy glow of their contents staggered her mind. The lantern light beamed off an empire's ransom of gold ingots and yard-long bars of silver, all appearing to be stamped with the official seal of their country of origin. Spanish doubloons, French francs, and even a crate filled to the brim with thousands upon thousands of copper coins added to the dazzling display.

It was treasure beyond her wildest imaginings.

She turned back to quiz him about what she'd just seen.

"Your eyes are as large and bright as medallions," he said with a smile.

"I'm sure," she agreed, and then made a sweeping motion with her arm. "Are you claiming that you took all that off the *James Bond*?"

"Every bit of it," he confirmed.

"It's a veritable fortune," she said, more to herself than to him.

"A half-million British pounds, give or take a few hundred thousand."

The sum so astounded Victoria that it took a real effort to find her voice. She drew in a deep breath, trying to regain her bearings. "Where did the *James Bond* get all this, anyway?"

"Veracruz."

She could hardly believe her ears. "Mexico?"

"They loaded it up before they set out for Martinique." He slipped a chain full of keys over his head. "It was bound for Spain."

"Spain?" she repeated, reeling at this new revelation. "But the *James Bond* was going to England."

"Eventually, perhaps. But the gold and silver were going to Spain." Crouching down, he used the keys to begin closing and locking the chests.

She frowned, trying to make sense of it all. "What was it going to be used for?"

He glanced back over his shoulder as he locked the last crate. "It was meant to help finance the Spanish-French armada in their coming fight against the British Navy."

Thoroughly confused now, she shook her head and said, "Surely our captain didn't know what was in the crates."

"Of course he knew."

"But he was English."

"So?" He seemed amused by her statement.

Angered by his attitude, she answered his question with one of her own. "So why would he agree to help the enemy?"

He stood and delivered yet another stunning bit of news. "Because your captain was a traitor. Had he lived, he would have collected quite a large, ill-gotten fee—not only for the treasure you've just seen, but also for selling the passengers on his ship into slavery."

For a moment her mind went blank. The captain of the *James Bond*—a traitor? And a slave trafficker as well! It was almost too much to comprehend. She met the pirate captain's straightforward gray gaze and, slowly, her head cleared and cold reality set in. Her captor might actually have been her savior.

"How do you know all this?" she finally asked him.

He shrugged. "Seaports are dens of gossip."

She looked at him speculatively. His buccaneer's attire aside, he seemed to be too clean, too much of a gentleman to be a pirate. Especially a pirate who hung about seaports and smugglers inns. His high-boned face held something gravely intelligent, even aristocratic, and his speech was refined, although his voice carried that slight hint of an accent that was not solidly British.

"Are you English?" she asked him, curiosity getting the better of her.

He didn't answer at first and she wasn't sure he had heard. Before she could ask again, he said, "Half English, half Sicilian—the dangerous half."

"What do you mean by that?"

"Time to go back up," he said, ignoring her question.

She tried again. "What's your name?"

He shot her an impatient look as he grabbed the dangling end of the rope.

"My name is Victoria," she persisted. "Victoria Gordon."

"Luca—my name is Luca," he finally relented.

She brightened at this small breakthrough. "Luca what?"

He handed her the rope. "Luca is enough. I'm not planning to have calling cards printed any time soon, and you won't have need to introduce me to anyone."

"I'm sorry," she said. "I know it's not polite to ask so many questions, but—"

"I've faced worse interrogations." Once she had the rope in hand, he gave it a yank to signal the sailor holding the other end.

She wondered what he meant by that but didn't have a chance to ask him anything else because the sailor began pulling her up.

"Kick off your shoes so they don't fall off and hit me again," Luca instructed. "I'll bring them up with me."

Not until she was halfway out of the hold did it occur to Victoria to question why Luca would care that the treasure he had captured was meant to help defeat the British Navy.

Was he really a pirate?

Or was he a patriot in disguise?

# Chapter 13

The Admiral removed the spyglass from his eye and glanced at Henry, who'd been standing beside him at the rail for the last hour or so. "How is your pirate faring?"

"My—" Henry ran a hand through his dark windswept hair and wondered to whom the older man was referring. Then it finally dawned on him. "Are you talking about Odd the Vonck?"

"None other." The Admiral nodded.

"He's not exactly *my* pirate." Henry couldn't resist pointing out. "He was, in fact, yours first."

"Until he slipped away with Dos Sebastián," the Admiral replied ruefully.

Henry remembered that night only too well. The decks of the pirate ship were awash with English sailors when Vonck and the Spaniard had escaped over the side and into the jolly boat, abandoning both ship and crew. The remaining pirates, sensing the battle was lost, scurried to hide, to no avail. Fear of the gallows rippled through their ranks as they were rounded up below the forecastle to await their fate.

The Admiral must have seen the fear in Henry's eyes when he inspected the line of shackled pirates he would soon be sentencing to death. Visibly surprised to find a such a young boy in the ranks of his captives, the older man had taken a closer look at Henry's face, badly bruised beneath the dirt and the soot and the blood. He'd ordered the rest of the prisoners locked down in the hold until he could conduct their trials and then he'd taken the boy aside to ask his name, his age, and how he'd come to be on the pirate ship.

Once the pirates were hanged but before the naval ship reached the shores of England, the Admiral had taken Henry under his wing, and then into his home and raised him like his own son.

"To answer your question, Odd the Vonck remains in sick bay," Henry said.

The older man let out a snort. "Good place for him."

"His face is still a bruised and bloody mess, and his broken arm is in a sling."

"Can't say I feel sorry for him."

"He's also vowing to send Dos Sebastián to Davy Jones's locker if we find him."

"Oh, we'll find him." The Admiral snapped his spyglass back up to his face to continue peering at the horizon across the white-capped waves. "And when we do, we had also better find that Miss Priss hasn't suffered so much as a splinter in her little finger."

A small smile curved Henry's lips as he touched the lace of her shawl, which he'd retied about his waist that morning when he'd bathed and changed clothes. Priss was no helpless debutante, all niminy-piminy and with no life beyond the next ball or dinner party. She was smart and sassy and perfectly capable of fighting back if the occasion warranted. Knowing her as well as he did, he was certain she had put up quite the struggle when the Spaniard's men grabbed her. He could just see her, kicking and biting and punching and clawing, perhaps even stealing one of her captors' knives and stabbing him.

"As for your pirate," the Admiral said, "he'll have to get in line."

"Indeed he will," Henry replied as he squinted into the streaming white sunlight.

The two men stood silently at the rail for a while, both thinking of Priss but from different perspectives, until shouts and curses on deck signaled there was trouble on board.

Turning, Henry shaded his eyes with both hands, looked aloft and saw the problem. A sailor was struggling with a torn royal. A rope had broken and the canvas it attached had flapped in the wind until it caught on the topgallant mast. It couldn't be lowered without tearing further, and sails were too costly and canvas too scarce on the open water to let that happen.

He knew the solution, because the same thing had happened once when he was serving as Dos Sebastián's cabin boy. The man in the ropes needed to shinny on up to the topgallant and push the royal over. If he couldn't do it, Henry would have to order another, more nimble sailor to climb up there and get it done.

"Well, back to work." Henry pushed up the sleeves of the tan shirt he'd found in Vonck's slop chest. Paired with the dark brown breeches he'd also discovered there, he was comfortably clad for his role as acting captain.

"Better clear the decks, while you're at it."

Henry turned back to the Admiral, who was still outfitted in his naval uniform. It looked worse for the wear in the sticky summer heat, but he'd refused to change out of it. "Why?"

The Admiral adjusted his glass, stared skyward and said, "We're in for a bad blow."

But all Henry saw when he frowned up at the sky was one distant white cloud that appeared to portend clear sailing ahead. He turned a bewildered gaze toward the older man, wondering if he was simply seeing things. Still, after he helped remedy the sail situation, he ordered the decks cleared . . . just in case.

Henry was so busy setting up watches and overseeing the other normal routines of keeping the ship on course that the Admiral's storm prediction slipped his mind. But as the afternoon scuttled toward twilight, the weather changed—and not for the better.

Vast black clouds blotted out the last light of dusk, bringing with them the wet-salt tang of rain. The wind came up, hard and fast. Singing and shrieking, it filled the sails with such violence that they strained and whined and stretched in turn. The seas roughened, and soon the ship was rolling and heaving in the dark foaming waves like a harpooned whale.

"All hands! All hands!!" the Admiral commanded from the poop deck.

The clanging of the ship's bell added an urgent note to his demand.

"Reduce sail! Stow cannons! Batten down the hatches!" The Admiral was clearly in his element, his voice ringing out louder and more vigorously than Henry had heard it in years as he bellowed out orders over a cacophony of cold blue lightning and crashing thunder. He continued bawling out orders as the rain poured down in needle-sharp torrents and the wind-driven waves washed across the decks—one so mammoth that it sent a sailor screaming to his death in the furious depths of the sea.

Henry was half drowned himself, his

hair plastered to his forehead and his shirt and breeches soaked through and clinging to his skin in dripping folds. He gladly relinquished command of the ship to the Admiral so he could help the crew close the hatches to prevent water from getting in below. He lashed down tarpaulins, reefed the mainsail to keep the ship from capsizing, secured the cannon carriages so they wouldn't crush anyone if they broke away, tied the ship's small boats more firmly in place—all in an effort to keep injuries to a minimum and the ship afloat.

His hatred of the sea doubled and then redoubled as he worked, and his muscles ached and bunched from both exhaustion and the wind-driven rain. But staying busy kept Henry from thinking about Priss. Was she riding out this very same storm aboard Dos Sebastián's ship?

*If she survives,* he thought during a moment of rest . . . *hell, if I survive—*

Another blaze of lightning followed by an explosion of thunder snapped him back to the task of splinting a young sailor's forearm, broken when a fierce gust of wind blew him out of the lower rigging and onto the deck. The ship's doctor had his hands full with other sailors who'd suffered more serious injuries, so it had fallen to Henry to set the boy's fracture.

"You're lucky it was a clean break," he told his patient as he wrapped one of several surprisingly clean bandanas that he'd found in Vonck's belongings around the flat pieces of wood he'd found to immobilize the broken limb. "Luckier still that you weren't killed."

"I thought sure I was a dead man when I fell." The ashen-faced youth tried to smile through his pain, and it was a pitiful sight to behold.

Dead *boy* was more like it, Henry thought as he fashioned a sling from the last bandana. He was thirteen, fourteen at the most. Henry was tempted to ask him why he'd run off to sea instead of staying home, going to school, and eating his mother's cooking. Had someone, his father perhaps, beaten him? Or had he, like Henry, been kidnapped off the street and sold to the highest bidder?

Not that it mattered at this point. The boy was here, he was hurt, and he'd taken his medical treatment like a man.

Finished splinting and slinging, Henry conducted a final check to make sure that the broken arm was set firmly but not so tightly that it cut off circulation. Satisfied that it was done correctly, he turned to the old tar standing behind him and ordered, "Pass me the rum."

"I—I don't drink, sir," the boy protested when Henry put the flask to his trembling lips.

"Doctor's orders," Henry shoved the youngster's head back and made him drink. "It'll help with the pain."

The young man choked, then swallowed until half the flask was empty.

"Good lad," Henry said. "Now go find a vacant hammock and try to get some sleep."

"I'll try, sir." His patient winced at the spit of salt-tinged rain buffeting his rum-flushed face. "But I'm guessin' there'll not be much sleep for anyone tonight."

*The Caribbean*

Victoria was sound asleep when thunder boomed, loud as a cannon, waking her with a start. She opened her eyes just as a jagged streak of lightning illuminated the dark cabin. The wind came up, lashing at the ship and causing it to pitch feverishly. Rain began pouring down, pelting the diamond-paned windows so hard she feared the glass would break.

The ship's bell was struck repeatedly to call the alarm.

Forcing down her panic, Victoria said a quick, heartfelt prayer. Then she took a shaky breath of the steamy, stale cabin air, pulled the quilt up as far as she could and wrapped it tightly around her. When the ship lurched ominously, she clutched the side of her berth to keep from being thrown out and onto the floor.

Lightning flashed again, followed by another bellow of thunder.

Victoria pulled the pillow over her head, trying to drown out the wailing of the wind, the drumming of the rain, along with the running footsteps and shouted orders from the men on deck fighting for their lives against the awesome power of nature.

She stayed like that, a shaking ball of fear, for hours that seemed like years.

Finally, the storm abated. The wind died down, so low that that it simply rocked the ship in a gentle motion. The sounds of footsteps and shouting faded away. The rain dwindled to a soothing pitter-patter.

Victoria was just beginning to drift off back to sleep, mercifully lulled by the blessed quiet, when the cabin door banged open. Startled anew, she peeked out from her cocoon and saw the silhouette of a man, backlit by the passageway lantern, standing in the open doorway. He said nothing, but she knew it was Luca.

She wanted to ask him what he was doing here. A ridiculous question given that this was his cabin. She wanted to tell him she wasn't afraid. An idiotic thing to say considering she was still covered up and cowering in his bed. Instead, she just froze in place and hoped he wouldn't realize she was awake.

He stepped into the cabin, hung his oilskin slicker on a peg, and closed the door. The smell of stormy skies and salty seas clinging to his hair and his skin trailed him as he strode silently past her to the other side of the cabin. He pulled some blankets out of one of the drawers and made a rude pallet of them on the floor not far from her berth.

"Go back to sleep, Victoria," Luca said as he laid down on the blankets.

It was the first time he'd spoken her name, and there was something in his soft, slightly accented pronunciation of it that made her heart skip a beat. Suddenly she felt safe and warm, comforted by his presence in the cabin in a way she didn't quite understand. She closed her eyes. The watchman on deck called out the midnight hour as she fell into a deep, dreamless sleep.

*Chapter 14*

⁓

$\mathcal{S}$leep was impossible.

Priss tossed and turned for what seemed like hours, unable to sleep in the throes of the storm. Finally, her head threatening to burst from the doleful clanging of the ship's bell, she got up and dressed, preparing to abandon ship if it became necessary. She was more cautious than afraid. She'd weathered numerous storms both at home and on her sailboat, but this was the loudest one she'd ever experienced.

The wind shrieked like a thousand battling stallions—whining, screaming, thudding. Wind-lashed rain beat down and foaming waves surged up from the turbulent sea to pound relentlessly at her window. The ship creaked and rocked and shuddered. Boards popped and rivets flew. Then, with the wild sound of thunder all around, there was a terrible ripping sound.

The mainsail? Priss staggered across the swaying floor of the cabin, thinking she would go up on deck to see if that's what happened. It was difficult to see where she was in the darkness. Before the storm struck, Tommy had put out the lantern lest the oil spill and cause a fire. Now a jagged blaze of lightning illuminated the cabin, providing enough brightness to guide her toward the door.

A thud and a bang behind her spun her around. In another flash of lightning she saw that the table where she ate and wrote was still standing but the chair had toppled and been flung across the cabin, coming to rest against the far wall. Fortunately, her pen and ink pot were safe, stored in the extra chamber pot Tommy had brought her, and she always tucked the pages she'd written under the bed covering before turning down the lantern and retiring for the night.

Priss started back across the cabin, intending to set the chair aright. The ship rolled, first one way and then the other, and she grasped the edge of the table to help her keep her footing. She held on until the ship settled a bit and then started toward the upturned chair again. Suddenly a roaring gust of wind hit the ship, causing it to heave. Rather than turn back and try to grab the table again, Priss grabbed at the chair to stay upright, missed, and fell backwards.

Pain exploded as the back of her head hit the hard floor. The ceiling blurred and then faded. Her head spun, her eyes closed. Awash in pain and darkness, she passed into  oblivion . . .

The first thing she saw when she finally opened her eyes were pale pink streaks of dawn streaming in through the window. How long had she been unconscious? She closed her eyes, wondering, and laid perfectly still as her mind began to clear and her senses to sharpen. She heard the cabin door open and close, but couldn't summon enough energy to see who had come in.

"Miss Priss!" Tommy cried. "Wake up! What happened? Are you all right?"

She opened her eyes again and saw his frightened, chalk-white face looming over her. "I—"  She drew in a deep breath and winced at the pain in her head. "I think so, yes."

"Do you need a drink o' water? A glass o' wine?" He sounded anxious to fetch one or the other, perhaps both, for her.

"Not now, Tommy." Priss gave him a trembling smile. "But thank you."

"A wet cloth? Breakfast?"

"No breakfast." The thought of food at this moment made her stomach turn. "But I do need you to help me sit up."

Tommy grasped her outstretched hand and gently pulled her to a sitting position.

Priss waited for the vicious bout of dizziness that assailed her to pass. When it finally did, she touched the throbbing knot on the back of her head. She was afraid that she might find she had been badly injured, but she had to know one way or the other. Relief poured through her when she brought her fingers to the front and saw no blood on them.

She could hear hurried footsteps racing past her cabin door and up the steps. From the deck came the sounds of shouting and cursing interspersed with moans and groans of pain. No sooner had she assimilated all that than it occurred to her that that the ship was dead in the water.

"We're not seaworthy, are we?" she asked Tommy.

A frown crumpled his face. "The rudder broke when we were steering into the storm. Cap'n said if it can be pieced together today, we can limp to the nearest port in the morning."

"What is the nearest port?"

"Vigo."

"Spain." Priss remembered reading about the Battle of Vigo Bay during the War of Spanish Succession, and the great victory led by the English Admiral George Rooke. "Why there?"

"It's the Cap'n's home port, so he knows where to get what he needs to repair the ship proper." Tommy brightened then. "Plus, he can get some more o' them good oranges."

"How long will it take us to get there?"

"A half day or so."

"And how long after that to Algiers?"

"Another week?" His guess sent chills through her.

"All right, Tommy." Priss forced herself first to her knees, where she remained until she regained her equilibrium, and then got to her feet.

"Let's to up on deck to see what's happened to the ship."

"You can't go topside." He looked shocked at the idea.

Priss frowned at him. "Why not?"

"'T'aint proper for a lady like yourself t' be mixin' with the sailors," he lectured her.

"I'm not planning to 'mix' with them," she argued.

"'Sides," he added, "women are supposed t' be bad luck on board, and the crew might blame you for the storm."

"I'm not here of my own volition," she reminded him.

He looked at her blankly.

"I'm not here because I want to be," she clarified. "Your captain's men kidnapped me."

"Aye," he conceded, "but there's no tellin' what they'll do with you or to you if they see you on deck."

Priss acknowledged he had a point, but she was dying to leave the cabin after being locked up for a week. She looked him over, sizing him up, an idea forming. "Tommy, do you have a jacket or an overshirt I can borrow?"

He hesitated. "A jacket, yes, but—"

"And socks," she added. "I'm a little

taller, but not much bigger than you. I'm sure your jacket will fit me."

He eyed her dubiously.

She nodded, her mind made up. "Go get the jacket."

"You should eat somethin' first," he protested.

"I'll eat when we get back," she promised.

Seeming to realize the futility of arguing with her, he spun on his heel and left the cabin. He returned shortly with a roughly woven jacket. Priss put the jacket on over her shirt and knee breeches and was pleased to find that it was baggy enough to almost obscure the curves of her figure.

But her hair! What to do with her hair?

"Do you have a hat?"

"In one o' the pockets."

She dug in the pockets and found his knit hat. It took some doing, especially with the throbbing knot on the back of her head, but she finally managed to wind her hair into a tight bun on top of her head and then yanked the hat on over it.

Worry wrinkled Tommy's brow when she was finished.

She looked at him askance. "What's the matter?"

"You still look too . . ." He struggled to find the right word. "Girly."

She turned up the jacket collar to hide the bottom half of her face. "How's this?"

"Better," he said, and opened the door. "Now keep quiet and stay behind me. If the Cap'n sees us skulking around, there'll be the Devil to pay."

Priss could hear banging and sawing and cursing on the deck above as she followed Tommy out of the cabin and up the steps. None of it boded well for what awaited them topside. Still, it was the first time she'd had a breath of fresh air since the evening she was kidnapped, and she gloried in it. The swell had died away, leaving the flotsam-covered sea curiously still, and the bright sun and white clouds promised a much better day.

The delight she took in the nice weather faded quickly when she peeked around Tommy's shoulder. It shocked her to see the devastation from the storm. The ship was drifting aimlessly on the water, crippled without a functioning rudder. Frayed ropes and rigging lines snaked haphazardly across the rubbish-strewn deck. The mainsail was ripped, accounting for the tearing sound she'd heard during the storm, and several smaller sails were torn and hanging limply from the overhead spars.

Dos Sebastián stood on the poop deck, too busy shouting orders and cursing his crew to notice her and Tommy standing in the shadows. The pirates scurried to perform their tasks under the Spaniard's verbal lashing. Some were carrying boards and nails to fix the rudder. Others were either splicing the ragged ends of two pieces of rope together with wooden fids to replace the lost rigging or patching the torn sails with extra pieces of canvas. Still others were clearing the deck by throwing most of the debris overboard.

Almost as bad as the wreckage were the injuries that many of the crew members appeared to have sustained during the storm. Several of them wore blood-soaked bandages around their heads or slings to support broken arms or wrists. A few were either limping cautiously across the still-wet deck or leaning heavily on makeshift walking sticks. One young pirate, more boy than man, sat in the shadows of the bulkhead, bent forward, in obvious pain as he cradled a hand with swollen, blackened fingers against his stomach.

"Did anyone die?" she asked Tommy.

He turned his head and looked out at the hostile sea. "A couple men washed overboard."

Priss wasn't surprised, given the ferocity of the storm.

"Cap'n said we don't have time to search for their bodies."

That didn't surprise her, either. Dos Sebastián was too self-absorbed to care about anyone else, even those who had died trying to save his ship. He probably regarded their watery deaths as a personal insult.

"'Sides," Tommy added on a forlorn sigh, "the sharks probably got 'em."

Rather than dwell on that grisly thought, Priss focused her attention on the sound of incessant banging. "What's that noise?"

"The jolly boat hittin' against the hull," Tommy said.

She stood on tiptoe, trying to get a look over the side, but she wasn't close enough to see anything. "What happened to it?"

"The ladder came loose during the storm."

"How will they fix it?"

Tommy shrugged. "They'll throw one o' the spare ladders over the side, like they're going to climb down into the boat, but they'll stay on the ladder to repair the davits and tighten the ropes."

A thought flashed through Priss's mind: *If she could just get into that jolly boat . . .*

She'd often heard her father say that the most daring act was usually the most successful. She hadn't really understood at the time, but she did now. She would keep her father's advice firmly in mind during the next two days. If any situation appeared beyond hope, it was her being able to escape from this ship before it reached Algiers.

"How many jolly boats are there?" she asked, trying not to sound as devious as she suddenly felt.

"One on each side of the stern, and a couple o' pinnaces—" Tommy cast a suspicious glance at her. "Why're you askin' me that, anyway?"

She shrugged. "I'm just curious."

He regarded her sternly. "If you're thinkin' what I *think* you're thinkin'—"

"Of course not." But she didn't even sound convincing to her own ears.

By the time Tommy took her back to the cabin and left to get her something to eat, Priss had already decided that she was going to escape. She wasn't sure how she would manage it, but she realized that her best chance would be when they anchored off Vigo sometime tomorrow. Which meant there was little time to waste and much to be done.

Once the ship was under sail again, she'd send word to Dos Sebastián that she needed to ask him a few questions for the story he thought she was writing about him. She was sure that would pique both his interest and his ego. Her questions would be about simple things, like when and where the watchmen were posted, how high the crow's nest was, and what he considered his most successful treasure haul.

Those questions would lead to the one she really wanted to ask, which was how he'd managed to jump ship after her father had arrested him. She'd have paper and pen at the ready, for it was imperative that she write down exactly what he told her. Some small detail in his answer might supply her with the ways and means to accomplish her own escape.

She was still at the Spaniard's mercy, of course, so she would have to be shrewd in phrasing her questions so as not to arouse his suspicions. In spite of her apprehension, she couldn't help but smile. She would flatter him, praise his cunning and his audacity. Vainglorious as he was, he likely wouldn't doubt her intentions and would instead sing his own praises.

Setting up the chair that had toppled over during the storm, Priss climbed up on it and looked out the window that she wiped clean every morning and evening in hopes of spotting an approaching ship.

She hadn't given up on Henry, but it was fast becoming clear to her that she couldn't just sit around waiting for him to come to her rescue. If he didn't arrive today—or tomorrow, at the latest—she might well wind up on an Algerian auction block before the week was out.

She hoped to convince Tommy to come with her, thus freeing him from a life of servitude at sea. He was young and smart and trustworthy, and deserved a better future than he would have if he remained under the Spaniard's boot. But whether Tommy decided to stay or to go with her, she was determined to get off this ship and go home.

A ball of ice formed in her stomach when she saw triangular fins break the surface of the water. The sharks would probably follow the ship to Spain as a sort of macabre clean-up crew. They were but one of the dangers she'd face when she made her move.

Priss knew she would have to be as careful as she was clever. She couldn't let fear cloud her mind or cause her to falter. If she should fail to escape when they got to Vigo, she wouldn't get a second chance.

———∼∽∼———

Conducting a quick survey in the morning light, Henry was pleasantly surprised to see how well Vonck's ship had weathered the storm. Several sails had had to be patched, some of the ropes and the torn and sagging rigging replaced, and debris removed from the deck. But overall, the ship had survived the worst of Mother Nature's wrath in pretty good shape.

He gave the credit to the Admiral's unexpectedly accurate forecast, which allowed the crew time to prepare for the tempest, and to the helmsman's ability to turn into the storm and sail at an angle along the waves with the stern, the strongest part of the ship, taking the brunt of their force. Together, they had saved the ship and all but that one crewman who had washed overboard.

"Assessing the extent of damages?" the Admiral asked as he joined him at the rail.

"It's not nearly as bad as I'd expected," Henry said.

The Admiral's uniform had gotten soaked in last night's storm, and he'd hung it on hooks in the captain's cabin when he'd finally retired. This morning it was still too damp to wear, so he'd reluctantly donned a long-sleeved shirt and a pair of trousers that Henry had found at the bottom of one of the sailors' sea chests. The civilian attire aside, he still exuded an air of military authority.

He extended his ever-present spyglass and let out a long, low whistle. "Will you look at that?"

Henry shaded his eyes against the

prickly glare of sun on sea. "What is it?"

"Flotsam from last night's storm."

Just then Henry saw part of a mast float by, washing clear out to sea. He stared at it dumbly for a few seconds before it hit him. "You don't suppose that's from—?"

"The Spaniard's ship?" The Admiral nodded. "I'd bet my remaining years on it."

A broken chair drifted past and then a bare foot—a man's foot, judging by the size of it. He said to the Admiral, "Assuming it survived the storm—"

"Another good bet."

"Where is it now?"

The Admiral folded up the spyglass. "Probably hobbling toward the nearest port."

"Which is . . .?"

"Vigo."

Henry's head jerked around. "Spain?"

The Admiral rubbed the eye that had spent the better part of the week against a spyglass. "I studied Vonck's charts before I came topside this morning. Despite his messy personal appearance, his records are quite orderly."

Henry waited mutely while the older

man used the astrolabe he'd found on the pirate's desk to determine the ship's latitude.

"We made good time until the storm," the Admiral finally said. "Now we're half a day, or less, from Vigo."

"And Dos Sebastián's home port." Henry was surprised to realize he remembered that from his cabin boy days.

"Exactly." The Admiral breathed in deeply and smiled. "Ahhh, I can smell the orange trees and the olive groves from here."

Henry turned, cupped his hands around his mouth and called, "*Helmsman!*"

Enda McKenzie raised his thick red brows and called back, "Aye, sir?"

"Change of direction."

"Where to, sir?" the Scotsman asked.

"Vigo," Henry ordered.


*The Caribbean*

Victoria woke up to a stream of sunlight spilling in through the cabin windows. Remembering the violence of last night's storm and her uninvited but very welcome guest, she rolled over to find that Luca and his blankets were gone and she was now alone. She sighed, unsure if she was relieved or disappointed, and then threw back the covers intending to get up and get dressed.

A knock on the door had her covering back up for modesty's sake.

"Come in," she called, hoping it was Luca.

Her hopes were dashed when she saw it was the doctor.

"Good morning, Lady," he said as he carried her breakfast tray into the cabin. He crossed to the desk and set it down, then turned and asked her, "The storm kept you awake?"

She realized he didn't know that Luca had slept on the floor last night, and prayed he didn't notice the warm flush that crept up her cheeks. "It did at first," she admitted. "But then I managed to sleep quite well. I just woke up, in fact."

The doctor nodded his approval. "You would like a bath before you disembark this afternoon?"

His question rendered her speechless. Finally, she managed to ask, "Disembark?"

"We close to de island where de passengers will be released."

"Including me?" She wanted to make doubly sure it was so.

"Including you," he confirmed.

More surprising than his news was the strange mixture of anticipation and dread that claimed her. On the one hand, she was delighted to hear that she was going to be released. On the other hand, she realized that she wasn't quite ready to say goodbye to Luca.

Luca. Dark, mysterious, and—

"You are unhappy?" the doctor asked, concern threading his voice.

Startled by his question, Victoria looked up.

"You are frowning."

She forced a smile. "I'm happy. Truly. I'm happy to know that I'm going home to England and that I'll soon be seeing my father again."

"But?" he prompted as her smile faded.

She couldn't tell him the real reason she was conflicted, so she came up with a plausible excuse. "But I'm worried what the other passengers will say when I show up on deck after being away from them all this time. How will I explain—?"

"Not to worry." He waved away her concern. "One of de women asked about you. Her husband was killed during the attack."

Victoria wondered if that woman was the frothy wife of the portly man who had died rescuing her from that pirate's clutches. "What did you tell her?"

"I told her you were hurt and under my care."

"Did she believe you?"

"Enough so as to share it with de other passengers."

Relief trickled through her. "Thank you."

"Now," he said as he made to leave the cabin, "a bath and clean clothes and you will be ready to leave in a few hours."

"Doctor," she called after him.

He turned at the door. "Yes?"

"Will . . . " She paused, trying to think of how to phrase her question, then took a deep breath and plunged on. "Will the captain speak to us before we disembark?"

"No, Lady." He gave his grizzled head a brisk shake. "De captain has a ship to run and other duties to attend to."

Victoria had hoped to be able to say goodbye to Luca, if for no other reason than to hear him say her name one more time. But now she cleared her throat, trying not to let her disappointment show, and nodded. "Of course he does."

"De crews of de two boats know what to do and where to go," he told her before he opened the door and left the cabin. "Dey will get you all set up—help you sharpen sticks to catch fish and start de fire so you can cook dem, show you where to sleep and bathe and dress—before dey come back to de ship."

While the doctor arranged for her bath and sought out some other clothes, Victoria ate her breakfast. By the time she finished eating and bathing and donning another clean but musty-smelling striped shirt and a pair of too-big breeches that she again fastened around her waist with the tail of the shirt, it was almost noon.

She sat on the edge of the bed, her hands folded in her lap and her toes curled to keep the too-big shoes from falling off her feet. She was still torn.

On the one hand, she didn't want to leave without saying goodbye to Luca. On the other hand, this might be the only chance she would ever have to go back to London, to go back to her family and her friends, to go back to life as she had always known it.

Besides, according to those two sailors who'd followed behind her to the hold, women were considered bad luck on board a pirate ship—meaning the crew would probably be glad to be rid of her and the other women.

As for Luca ... well, her imagination had already run wild once, when he'd caught her around the waist and lowered her gently to the floor of the hold. His dancing gray eyes had smiled into hers, and had left her warm and wanting for she knew not exactly what. But it didn't matter now, because she was leaving. And that was that. Luca was a pirate, she reminded herself. For all she knew, he might have a wife and a half-dozen children stowed away somewhere. Or, worse, he might have a woman in every port.

Looking down at her attire, a smile curved Victoria's lips at the thought of how polite London society would react if they could see her now, wearing a man's shirt and breeches instead of a dress. She couldn't help, then, but picture the shocked expression on the faces of her father and her friends when they learned that she had been living in Luca's cabin and that they had spent the night together.

Just the two of them. Alone.

Of course, he had slept on the floor and she on the bed. And they both had been fully clothed and covered with blankets. But there was no question that in the eyes of that same London society she would be considered thoroughly compromised.

It suddenly occurred to her that neither her father nor her friends need ever know that any of it had happened. No one but Luca and the doctor and herself knew that she had spent her time in the captain's cabin. Both of them were staying behind, and she certainly wasn't going to tell—

A knock on the door interrupted her train of thought. She sat up straight, prepared, albeit reluctantly, to leave both the ship and Luca behind. "Come in."

"You are ready?" the doctor asked.

"Yes," she answered.

He handed her a folded red bandana

that looked very much like the one Luca had had tied around his hair the day he attacked the merchantman.

"What is this for?"

"You wear this on island to protect your hair from the sun."

"Thank you," she said, "I will."

"Captain has many." He got a crafty look in his eyes as he unwittingly confirmed her suspicion about the bandana's origin. "Won't miss just one."

Victoria put the bandana in her pocket. It was the only tangible memory she had of the time she had spent with Luca, and she silently vowed she would keep it safe in a drawer once she finally got home.

"I be back shortly," the doctor said as he picked up her breakfast tray and carried it away.

Blazing sunlight bathed Victoria's face in heat when she went up on deck to join the rest of the *James Bond's* survivors. Besides herself, there were three men, four other women, and several children, all dressed in similar fashion as she. One of the mothers carried a small bundle of whatever belongings she had managed to salvage, but the others stood empty-handed.

The face of the widow of the man who had died saving Victoria from that brigand's clutches clouded with anger when she aw her coming to join the other captives.

"Pirate's woman!" she hissed, pointing an accusatory finger.

Victoria felt hot color crawl up her face, but a response eluded her.

Spittle flew from the recent widow's mouth as she carried on. "I can't believe my husband died and this . . . this *pirate's woman* lived!"

The raucous laughter of circling gulls and the gentle ripple of wind in the sails was all that broke the stunned silence.

"That's what the crew calls you, you know. *Pirate's woman*," she jeered, the edge in her voice as wicked as the unrelenting sun. "Those sailors," she added loudly, "they gossip worse than backstairs servants."

Victoria could feel her composure slipping away like an eel in dark water. She glanced around, desperate to find either a champion or an escape from this horrible situation. But the sailors and the other survivors had backed away slightly and were simply staring at the two women.

A brawny sailor standing by the rope

ladder that had been thrown over the ship's side brought an end to the ugly situation when he ordered the group to climb down into the small boats that would take them to the island.

The men stepped aside to allow the women and children to go first.

Still reeling from the accusation that had been hurled at her, Victoria made the mistake of looking down when it was her turn to climb over the rail. The small boat appeared to be miles below her, and she could feel her hands growing clammy and her knees going wobbly.

The sailor grabbed her arm and said in a quiet voice, "Don't look down, Miss."

Victoria recognized him as the pirate who'd given her that very same advice just before she'd been lowered into the hold a week or so ago. She nodded weakly, wanting him to know she appreciated both his steadying hand and his hushed directive. She drew a deep breath and closed her eyes, willing the waves of dizziness to disappear. When they finally abated, she carefully climbed the rest of the way down. At last the floor of the boat was under her feet, and she took a seat back near the stern. To her relief, the widow who had unfairly blamed her for her husband's untimely death was in the other boat.

With a wooden creak of the oars and the soft rush of water sliding under the keel of the jolly boats, the sailors began rowing in tandem.

The small boat emerged from the shadow of the ship, bobbing on the water behind them. Victoria glanced back. It was the last time she would see the pirate ship. She should have been relieved. She was finally going home. Instead, she felt a surprising welter of emotions boiling up inside her, all of them centered on the man who was staying aboard.

Why were her thoughts so full of Luca—the smiles, the laughter, and what she had believed were the beginnings of an affectionate com-panionship? They were from two entirely different worlds. He was a pirate, an outcast, a man with no country who might soon be plundering other ships from her country, as well as those from Spain and France. She was a gently-reared Englishwoman whose life until now had consisted of a childhood in London, followed by years at the convent school in

Martinique, all in preparation of becoming a genteel wife and loving mother someday. They had no future as either lovers or friends, and she was foolish to fantasize otherwise.

Besides, she told herself as she lowered her head and forced herself to look resolutely forward, it wasn't like she would ever see him again.

In her mind's eye, though, there were pictures of him that would never be lost. She could see his feral smile that had filled her with such trepidation as he'd approached her on the day he had attacked the *James Bond*. Then the amusement that had glittered in his eyes and curved his lips when, hours later, she had looked up from the floor of his cabin and heard him ask if she wanted a bath. And she would never forget that devil's grin he'd flashed when he'd glanced down at her bare feet that day in the hold . . .

She could see them all as clearly now as she had then, and she would treasure those memories forever..

What Victoria didn't see because she didn't look back again was a grim-faced Luca standing on the forecastle deck, watching her boat disappear into the distance.

# Chapter 15

Within an hour of **Dos Sebastián's ship** dropping anchor off Vigo, Priss began putting her escape plan into action. She started with Tommy. He'd told her when he brought her dinner that the Spaniard had let part of the crew go into port and that they wouldn't be back until morning.

A stroke of luck, at last! she thought. There would be fewer pirates on board tonight to intercept her. When Tommy returned to remove her tray, she asked him to bring her his jacket and hat again as well as another pair of socks to pad her heels against those blistering shoes that cut at them.

His mouth popped open in surprise. "You're going topside?"

"Yes," she confirmed. "At midnight."

A quick expression of worry creased his youthful features. "Midnight?"

Priss decided to tell him the truth. "I'm going to escape tonight, and I need your help."

Tommy hesitated and seemed to debate something for a moment before he sighed and said, "I'll help you."

"I hope you'll come with me, too."

"Oh, no, Miss Priss, I—I can't."

Her hopes fell. "Why not?"

"The Cap'n'ld whip me into a bloody pulp and throw me to the sharks if he caught me." There was no mistaking the fear in his voice. "And there's no tellin' what he'd do to you."

"I have to get off this ship and go home, Tommy. My father is ill. He needs me. And if I do happen to get caught," Priss promised, "I swear I won't say a word about your helping me."

That seemed to be all the reassurance he needed. "I'll be back shortly."

It was a perfect night to escape. The sky was overcast with only a few feeble strands of moonlight filtering through the clouds. From her window Priss could see the dim outline of other ships buoyed in the bay and the glimmer of lights from the town beckoning several small boats in the water to come ashore. She took heart in the realization that no one would probably notice another small boat joining their fleet.

Tommy brought her the jacket, hat, and the pair of socks she had requested. He promised he would come back and guide her up to the deck a little before midnight. She put on the clothes, folded the pages she had written while on board ship into the pocket of her breeches, and sat down on the side of the bed.

And then she began to worry. Was she foolish to trust Tommy to assist her in escaping? Suppose he slipped up somehow and Dos Sebastián tortured the truth out of him? Or she accidentally stumbled in her thick socks and clumsy shoes and gave herself away? What would the Spaniard do to them?

She stayed on the bed, stewing in self-doubt, until she heard the watchman call out that it was half past eleven. A few minutes later came a stealthy tap on the door. Tommy looked in from the passageway and motioned for her to come with him. Her heart beat with both fervor and fear as she obeyed.

"I changed my mind," he said in a low voice. "I'm coming with you."

"You made the right decision," Priss told him and gave him a quick hug.

"I brought us some oranges," Tommy said, patting his pockets, "in case we get hungry before we get to town."

She followed him up the stairs to the deck, then stood in the shadows while he checked from side to side and from bow to stern to make sure they were in the clear. He waved to the man on watch, who returned the wave before turning away. Tommy took her by the elbow then and they hurried to the rope ladder left hanging over the side by the departing pirates.

Only to nearly bump into someone climbing up from a small boat drifting away from the pirate ship. A man, was all Priss could make out in the gleam of the moonlight on the water.

She let out a short, shocked scream and fell back, tugging Tommy with her.

The man swung nimbly over the side onto the deck. He wore a tan shirt, breeches, and tall boots. He had dark hair and—

Priss's mouth fell open.

"It's me," he said, clapping a hand over her mouth.

"Henry!" she cried, her voice muffled

by his hand, her heart leaping for joy at the sight of him.

"Henry?" Tommy echoed, sounding thoroughly confused.

"How did you find me?" Priss asked softly when Henry dropped his hand.

"I'll tell you when we're safely away," he whispered back.

"My father—?"

"He's waiting for you aboard our ship." His gaze slid to Tommy. "Who might this be?"

"A fellow prisoner." Priss clutched Tommy's shoulder as he tried to duck away. "His name is Tommy. He's a cabin boy, taken by the Spaniard just as you were."

"Well then." Henry smiled. "Would you like to come with us, lad?"

"I would, sir." Tommy nodded. "If it please ye."

"It pleases me a great deal," Henry said kindly. "Come along then."

"Who goes there?" a gruff voice shouted.

The three of them froze in place as light from a lantern raised by a grizzled pirate with no front teeth washed over them.

"Speak up, demme ye!" he ordered.

"What's all that noise?" the watchman bellowed down, loud enough to wake every sleeping soul still aboard ship.

*Oh, no!* Priss thought, her hopes sinking. *We're caught!*

Tommy shrank against her.

Henry muttered a curse and drew them both close.

The light flashed once more across the faces of Henry, Priss, and Tommy.

"Looks like we're bein' boarded," the grizzled pirate barked.

"The devil ye says!" the watchman bawled back in answer.

A gust of wind blew back the front of the knitted cap on Priss's head revealing her blonde hair.

"Blimey!" the pirate exclaimed. "It's that gel th' Cap'n had us grab!"

"She 'bout bit off me finger when we brought 'er aboard!" cried a sleepy-sounding pirate who had just joined them on deck.

"I tol' ye she were bad luck!" yet another pirate chimed in.

Henry stepped in front of Priss and Tommy, putting himself between them and the three pirates. Tommy tried to wiggle away, but Priss held him fast at her side.

"Looks like she's tryin' t' escape!"

The light swung in Tommy's direction. "And ye, ye slimy cur! Ye're 'elpin' 'er!"

The hideous clanging of the ship's alarm bell brought a dozen or more pirates, most carrying lanterns, racing up from their sleeping quarters and onto the deck. A few drew their swords or knives, others their pistols, all preparing to defend the ship. Curses and snarls and shouted threats added to the din and the confusion.

"*Silencio!*" Dos Sebastián's angry voice rang out, and the pirates quieted.

Henry remained standing in front of Priss and Tommy as the Spaniard, clad in what appeared to be a hastily-donned muslin shirt and black trousers, approached the trio.

"You will pay dearly for this betrayal," he hissed at Tommy. "Now get back to your duties."

Tommy blanched at the threat but stood his ground.

The Spaniard swung his attention to Henry. "And you are?"

"You don't remember me, I'm sure." Henry smiled, relishing the opportunity to finally confront his hated nemesis. "But many years ago I, too, was your cabin boy."

214

The Spaniard looked closer, his brows drawing together in perplexity.

"At least I was," Henry added, "until Admiral Robert Fitch rescued me."

Recognition flashed in Dos Sebastián's eyes. "Ah, I remember now. You were always a troublemaker. The one who stole food—"

"Because I was hungry."

"And blankets."

"I was cold."

"The one I had to beat—"

"The one who got away," Henry cut in coldly.

The pirate captain cocked his head far enough to the side to see Priss standing behind Henry. His mouth curved maliciously under the thick mustache. "And now you repay the Admiral by rescuing his daughter?"

"Soon to be my wife," Henry shot back.

Priss gasped in happy surprise. And with her next breath wanted to crown him for waiting until now—when they were surrounded by pirates and their lives were in danger—to declare himself.

"If you live long enough to marry her," the Spaniard said in a mocking tone.

"Meaning?"

"Meaning you must fight for her."

Henry accepted the challenge with an unwavering, "Gladly."

Dos Sebastián pointed to a member of his crew. "Bring the Toledo cutlasses from my cabin."

The pirate ran to do his bidding.

"And you, sand the deck," the Spaniard commanded another. "I don't want to be slipping in this sod's innards."

Priss slipped up beside Henry. He wore a grimly determined expression she'd never seen before. He caught her about the waist and pressed her to him. She turned her face to the shelter of his broad shoulder and said in a low voice, "He's vain and he's angry."

"Which means he's twice as likely to make mistakes," he replied under his breath.

The first pirate handed over the twin swords, their blades glinting wickedly in the light of a dozen lanterns. The second sanded a large circle on the deck, then both rejoined the rest of the crew, flocking like starlings around the two combatants. Bottles of rum passed from hand to mouth to hand. The noise level increased again as some of the encircling pirates started betting pieces of eight on how long the duel would last and whether the intruder would live to see the sun rise.

The tension was so strong, that Priss could barely stand it.

Henry released her and pushed her gently back to stand next to Tommy.

"Guard her with your life, lad," Henry told him with a look that made the cabin boy gulp.

"I will, sir," he promised with a swell of manly pride.

Henry tested his cutlass, one hand raised and the other gripping the hilt, and made a few exploratory slashes at the air. Satisfied with the weight and the feel of the sword in his hand, he gave the Spaniard a curt nod.

"When you're ready," he said.

The pirate lunged.

Henry sidestepped it easily, leaving his tracks in the sand. As the Spaniard's sword came slicing downward, he met it with an upswing in a practiced parry. The pirate pulled his sword back and slashed at Henry, who deflected the blow with an answering slash, the force of which sent a minor shock through him.

Priss could almost feel the impact

of the murderous blows the two men exchanged. She clapped a hand over her mouth to keep from crying out when the tip of Sebastián's blade cut through the sleeve of Henry's shirt, evoking a bright scarlet stain on his tan shirt and an equally vivid stripe on the skin of his sword arm.

The pirates howled with glee but fell silent when Henry countered their captain's next strike. He parried, feinted skillfully and caught his foe with his sword up. The pirate's blade slid along Henry's and bit into his fingers. Henry shifted his sword to his other hand long enough to wipe his bleeding knuckles on his breeches and then shifted the sword back to his fighting hand.

Silver sparks flashed as the tempered steel met tempered steel until, roaring with rage and frustration, the Spaniard stepped back, clutched the hilt of his sword with both hands and slashed madly at Henry's head.

Or, rather, where Henry's head *had* been. He ducked under the blow, and the cutlass whistled over him.

Priss had seen pirate's blow coming and had closed her eyes. But the clash of sword on sword told her that Henry was back in the fight. It was too much to take. She had to look.

A blood lust shone in the Spaniard's eyes as he attacked with a vengeance.

The encircling pirates howled with glee but fell silent when Henry's cutlass arced, catching his foe's and pointing it straight up.

The pirate captain and the former cabin boy he'd so mercilessly abused stood, eyes locked and swords crossed. They said nothing, but Priss could hear them breathing in broken syncopation. Finally Henry gave Sebastián a shove. He stumbled back, and Henry seized the advantage, slicing his sword across the brigand's muslin-covered shoulder, drawing both blood and vengeance.

The Spaniard eyed Henry with a cold, killing stare and came slashing forward, his sword a blur of motion that went up then came down and clashed into the blade of Henry's sword.

If the pirate expected him to fall back, he was sorely disappointed.

Henry met him blow for blow.

The clang of steel on steel, coupled with the deafening war cries of the Spaniard's crew, filled the air.

Tommy tugged at the sleeve of Priss's

shirt and pointed starboard. "Look, Miss Priss."

She did—and was astonished to see grappling hooks arcing toward the pirate ship from another vessel. The din of battle and the shouts of the crew had masked the scrape and thump of the other ship coming alongside. The hooks found purchase and a bridge of planks slid over the gap between the ships.

For a moment Priss feared they were being attacked by another pirate ship, but then she remembered Henry saying that her father was waiting for her on the boarding vessel and she gave a whoop of joy.

"We're saved, Tommy!" she exclaimed, giving him a hug. "We're saved!"

As she was turning her attention back to the swordfight, Priss caught a glimpse of a pirate on her right reaching for his sword as if he intended to give his captain a helping hand. She grabbed the sword of the closest pirate to her, and with a nonchalant flick of her wrist honed by years of practice, she poked the would-be combatant with the tip of the stolen sword. He looked down at the cold, sharp steel pressing into his ribs and, with a sigh of resignation, dropped his sword hand to his side.

The pirates booed when Henry's sword struck a blow that drove the Spaniard back—then cheered when their captain countered with a furious and forceful series of slashes that spun Henry's cutlass from his grip.

Priss flew to his side with the purloined sword. He snatched it from her and plunged back into the fight. The shouts of the crew rose to a blistering din as Henry and the Spaniard feinted, parried, and thrust again, their swords whipping and whistling and clashing again and—

And then came the blast of a gunshot.

In the shocked silence that followed, Dos Sebastián's eyes widened and his jaw dropped. His sword slipped from his grasp, and he grabbed his chest with both hands. He looked down in incredulity at the blood gushing from between his fingers. Slowly, as if he were a puppet whose strings were being lowered by gradual degrees, he crumpled facedown into the sandy circle on the deck.

Henry, breathing hard, his face streaked with sweat, turned away from the fallen pirate, trying to locate where the gunfire had come from. He blinked in disbelief when he saw Odd the Vonck standing on the planks connecting his ship with the Spaniard's. The one-eyed pirate still wore his broken left arm in a sling, and he held a smoking pistol in his right hand.

"Ye kilt 'im!" one of the Spaniard's crew members shouted at Vonck.

"An' proud t' 'ave done so!" he hollered back.

Suddenly a knife came flying out of the crowd of riled-up pirates. It found its target in Vonck's right arm, just below the shoulder. The force of it knocked the gun out of his hand and him off balance. He fought to stay upright but, instead, he fell over the side of the planking. His screams of fury and fear ended with a loud splash.

Another uproar began among the crew—bellows and shouts, crude laughter, and the shattering of bottles. Without the Spaniard to keep them in line, the pirates argued amongst themselves as to who would be the next captain. Yelling and shoving led to fighting, and the fighting to several men being thrown overboard by their crew mates.

Henry hustled Priss and Tommy across the wooden bridge onto Vonck's ship. The planks and grappling hooks were removed behind them and the two ships began to drift apart.

The Admiral had wanted to cross over to the Spaniard's ship, to confront him one last time after all these years. Instead, he'd followed Henry's order to remain on Vonck's ship and had kept an anxious watch at the rail. The instant he saw the three of them set foot on deck, a beaming smile replaced his frown.

"Priss!" he cried joyfully.

She ran to him and was swept up in his loving embrace. "Oh, Father!" She felt a swimming fogginess fill her eyes. "I'm so sorry I put you through all this worry."

"It doesn't matter now," he said in a soothing tone. "All that matters is that you are alive." He choked up then and glanced at Henry. "Thank you for saving my daughter."

Priss stepped out of her father's arms and turned to Henry, who stood a few feet away. "I believe you have a question for my father, do you not?"

"I do." He smiled, stepped forward and cleared his throat. "Sir, I would like to ask for your daughter's hand in marriage."

"It's about damn time." The Admiral's blue eyes twinkled as he looked at Priss. "And what say you, young lady?"

A smiling Priss closed the distance between herself and her beloved. She threw her arms around his neck and answered in a voice that reverberated through the years, "Kiss me, Henry."

And he did, right there in front of the Admiral and Tommy and a handful of gaping pirates who were no longer under Vonck's command. When they drew apart, he said, "I assume that's a yes?"

"Yes," she said, and kissed him again.

"Now I can die a happy man," the Admiral declared when they broke apart.

An idea took root as Priss looked from Henry to her father, and from her father to Tommy, who stood shyly to one side with the oranges he'd taken from the Spaniard's supply still bulging in his pockets.

She placed a hand on his shoulder and drew him forward.

"Father," she said thinking of the bright future awaiting the brave cabin boy once she introduced him to the best tutor in the known world. "I would like for you to meet the young man who took such good care of me after I was kidnapped . . ."

# Chapter 16

London, 1702

The last place Victoria wanted to be this evening was at Lady Fairchilde's ball. After spending a month on that deserted island with the other captives waiting to be rescued, she wasn't keen on the idea of entering a room crowded with gossipy acquaintances and curious strangers. The very thought of it gave her chills.

She had come up with a dozen excuses to decline the invitation, but her father was having none of it. She began with the most simple argument a woman could make. "I have nothing suitable to wear."

Andrew Gordon had responded by summoning a dressmaker and paying her an outlandish sum of money to create in record time a new and fashionable wardrobe for his beloved daughter.

"It's too soon," she'd tried next. "I've only been back in London for a little over a month."

"Which means it's time for you to assume your proper place in society," he'd countered.

She didn't want to assume her "proper place in society," at least not yet. She still needed private time. Time to completely set aside what she had seen and heard and experienced aboard the pirate ship.

Time to forget about Luca . . .

Victoria finally made what she believed to be her best argument. "Please understand, Father. I'm just not ready to face the crush of people who'll be craning their necks to get a closer look at the 'Pirate's Woman'."

Thanks to one of the gossipy women who'd been rescued with her, Andrew had heard her referred to in that way. It broke his heart to think how it must hurt and humiliate her, but he also felt it was important that she deal with it as soon as possible instead of letting it grow into a long-lasting scandal.

News that the survivors were on their way home had reached London via a message that arrived shortly before the British ship that had picked them up had docked at Southampton. He'd never forget how she looked when she disembarked wearing a faded red bandana tied around her sun-bleached hair, a shirt with washed-out stripes, and breeches—breeches!—along with a pair of badly-worn shoes that appeared to have her hobbling down the plank.

Setting aside the memory of her shocking appearance upon arrival, he'd laid a loving hand over the fist she had clenched in her lap. "You have to face them all eventually, Victoria."

"I know," she admitted glumly.

"And the sooner you do, the sooner you look them in the eye and dare them to defame you to your face, the sooner they'll move on to their next victim."

He'd been right, of course, and she'd reluctantly agreed to go.

"Now to find you an escort," he'd mused aloud.

"Edward?" She perked up at the idea of spending the evening with her favorite cousin, a successful wool manufacturer and fiercely determined bachelor, Edward Gordon.

"The last I heard Edward was still up in Yorkshire overseeing his mills and busy negotiating with his new business partner." Her father's brow furrowed in thought. "Why don't I arrange for Patricia Lymon and her son, Percy, to escort you?"

Victoria frowned, trying to place the names.

"Patricia and your mother went to boarding school together," he reminded her.

She nodded. "Am I correct in remembering that Mother once said she was rather high in the instep."

"That she is," he confirmed. "But she was always fond of your mother, and I'm sure she'll be more than happy to help ease your way into society."

"What can you tell me about Percy?"

"He's a bit portly, but he seems to be a decent enough fellow."

So it was that Victoria now sat at one of Lady Fairchilde's elongated, candlelit dinner tables between Percy Lymon, who was wolfing down partridge, mushrooms, and French peas as fast as the servant could dish them out, and Percy's mother, who had stuffed her rather plump figure into a garish green gown replete with frilly ribbons and bows that would have been better suited to a young girl's dress.

Patricia Lymon rinsed her fingertips in the silver bowl of almond water set by her plate and turned to Victoria, taking in the fragile blue moiré gown that clung to her bare shoulders and swelling bosom.

"That color certainly complements your brown hair and eyes, my dear." She looked across Victoria then and demanded of her gluttonous son, "Doesn't it, Percy?"

"Yes, Mother," he answered dutifully as he perused a platter of frosted fruits.

"Thank you," Victoria replied politely.

Mrs. Lymon's gaze narrowed, and the volume of her voice increased. "But that golden cast to your skin . . . it's from sun exposure during your time aboard that pirate ship, is it not?"

Victoria took a deep breath. She had to be very careful about what she said. She needed to make an explanation and it had to be the right one. It was the only way to stop the speculation.

"Actually," she said, falling back on the story that she and the ship's doctor had agreed upon, "I spent my time in sick bay and I didn't see the sun until the other captives and I were put ashore on the island from which we were rescued."

Mrs. Lymon's eyes widened with skepticism and her voice went up another notch as she sniped, "How fortunate for you."

"What do you mean?"

"Well, we all know what pirates do with their female captives."

Victoria reeled with shock. The woman sitting across from them emitted an audible gasp. An oblivious Percy popped a frosted grape into his mouth.

Taking notice of the curious looks now being directed at her from the other diners, Victoria decided it was time to put a stop to this Nosey Parker's questions and insinuations. She glanced around the vast dining hall, desperate to find an excuse, any excuse to escape, and spied her salvation in the person of her cousin standing near a table on the other side of the room.

Wrapping her silk shawl around her shoulders, she gave the malicious older woman a wickedly sweet smile and said, "I beg your leave, Mrs. Lymon . . . and Percy," she added belatedly. "I see my cousin Edward across the room, and I really should speak to him."

Mrs. Lymon puffed up with indignation when Victoria rose from the table.

Percy responded by raising his empty wine glass for a refill.

Victoria had almost reached Edward's table when she realized he was engaged in conversation with a man who was standing with his back to her. She stopped short, reluctant to interrupt, and took a closer look at the man with whom her cousin was talking. She couldn't see his face, but there was something about him that seemed strangely familiar to her.

He wore his dark hair tied back in a tidy queue. It brushed the richly-embroidered blue-and-gold collar of the blue waistcoat and matching trousers that were tailored to accommodate his broad shoulders, trim waist, and long legs. He gestured with his hand as if to make a point, and she saw lace at his wrist. When he chuckled, the sound of the deep and throaty rumble that she'd heard only once before traveled along her spine like a tender caress.

Edward spotted her at that same

moment and excused himself from the conversation. Smiling, he closed the distance between them and opened his arms to embrace her. "Cousin Victoria, how beautiful you look!"

She was enveloped in a fiercely loving hug that almost lifted her off her feet so she only heard rather than saw the other man clearing his throat.

Edward released her then and said, "Victoria, I want you to meet my new business partner, Duc Luca di Mileto."

Victoria turned and took in a sharp breath at the sight of Luca. Luca! She had thought she would never see him again, certainly not under these circumstances and most definitely not with his full name preceded by a title. Stalling for time, she tucked a strand of hair that had come loose back into the coil at her nape and tried to regain her composure.

Edward regarded her quizzically for a few seconds before turning his gaze on Luca, who appeared suspended between amusement and shock.

"Luca has recently left government service," her cousin explained while Victoria and Luca continued to stare at each other in disbelief. "He won't confirm it, of course, but rumor has it that he was doing some very dangerous work for the Crown."

Luca stood stoically, neither confirming nor denying Edward's statement.

Victoria was grateful for her cousin's conjecture as it gave her a little more time to adjust to the necessity of pretending that Luca and she were perfect strangers.

"Anyway," Edward continued, "as soon as Luca has settled into his London townhouse, his fleet of ships will begin transporting the wool I manufacture to the Americas and to the Far East."

"Miss Gordon," Luca said at last. He stepped forward, took her hand and bent over it. As he brushed a light kiss on Victoria's knuckles, a warm pleasure traveled from her fingers all the way to her heart, where it settled with a finality she knew she could no longer deny.

"I am honored to make your acquaintance, Duc di Mileto," she said, trying hard to keep her voice from revealing the surprise and the pure pleasure she felt at seeing him again..

Luca straightened, and his smoky

eyes twinkled with a mischievous glint. "And you are Edward's cousin?'

Victoria smiled at him, acknowledging the secret they shared. "I am."

In the adjoining ballroom, the orchestra began warming up.

"May I have the first dance?" he asked in that slightly-accented voice she had thought she would never hear again..

"Yes," she answered, hoping it would be the first in a forever of dances. "Yes, you may."

# Chapter 17

Cornwall
1818

Six months married and three months with child, Priss finished her breakfast of plain toast and unsweetened tea. The bland combination had helped to stave off her morning sickness enough that she decided she would go up to her study and work a bit.

Henry had eaten earlier and, after kissing her goodbye, had left for the law office he still kept in the village. After a simple marriage ceremony in the local chapel and a brief wedding trip to London, where they had spent some time with her four sisters and their families, they had decided to accept her father's invitation to live in his spacious house.

It had taken some adjustment on

everyone's part—her father's in accommodating a full house at his age; herself in sharing her life, her love, her office, and her bedroom suite with Henry; and Tommy's as he had moved into a comfortable room at the end of the hallway and begun relearning how to sleep in a real bed instead of a musty old hammock or the hard floor—but now they were one big, happy family.

As she neared the library, Priss paused. The door was slightly ajar, and she could hear her father quizzing Tommy on the book he'd just finished reading about the Battle of Vigo Bay and the fabulous fortune Queen Anne had won that historic day.

Memories of the many and varied lessons she'd learned in that very same library came flooding back. She laid her hand on the barely discernible swell of her belly and knew with an overflowing well of love and certainty that Tommy and her baby-to-be had given her father a whole new lease on life.

Upstairs, she sat down at her desk, dipped her pen into the inkpot, and wrote the two words that she had long been working toward:

**The End**

# About the Author

$\mathcal{F}$ran Baker is the bestselling author of eighteen novels and counting. She has also edited one nonfiction title. The titles and categories of her books follow this brief bio, and her "Coming Soon" after that. Fran invites readers to visit her website at http://www.FranBaker.com.

# Books by Fran Baker

## Contemporary Romance:
*When Last We Loved*
*Love in the China Sea*
*On Love's Own Terms*
*Seeing Stars*
*The Widow and the Wildcatter*
*King of the Mountain*
*San Antonio Rose*
*The Lady & The Champ*
*Romeo, Romeo*

## Historical Romance:
*Once A Warrior*
*The Talk of the Town*

## Regency Romance:
*Miss Francie's Folly*
*Pursuing Miss Pippa*
*Miss Rose and the Rakehell*
*Miss Antiqua's Adventure*
*Miss Sophie's Secret*
*Miss Chloe's Campaign*
*Miss Priss and the Pirate*

www.ingramcontent.com/pod-product-compliance
Lightning Source LLC
Chambersburg PA
CBHW020324200626

46814CB00006BB/2400